KISSIMMEE VALLEY MURDERS

Exploits of Rick Ulrich, Private Investigator and Florida Cracker.

BOYD R. CAMPBELL

Generic Copyright Insert // Zuul Aug 28, 2012

Copyright © 2012 Boyd R. Campbell

All rights reserved.

ISBN: 0615689868

ISBN 13: 9780615689869

Prologue

Boy, I'll be glad when the work day is over so I can go cat fish fishing to night. I need to relax and fishing does relax me like nothing else will. There goes the dinner bell so I can finally put up my tools, from caretaking of the Sun 'n Fun Camp for the Blind, and go have something to eat. I sure did get dirty today planting those azalea plants around the dining and activity hall. I'll need to wash up though before going for dinner.

He headed for his little cabin that is provided for the employee's, to wash and change into some clean clothes. After he did his grooming duties he walked out of his cabin in a long, loping stride. He is an awfully tall and Rangie sort, with long arms and long legs. He is almost bald with no facial hair.

He does have a nice grin most of the time and is a jovial fellow and is like by most his peers.

The dining and activity hall is where we have all our meetings with staff and others. The chow line was short and that allowed me to time to pick and choose just what he wanted for a change. He ate his meal and returned to his cabin for a nap before it was time to get his gear ready to go fishing about midnight.

He woke from his nap around eleven, washed his face to wake himself up and then gathered his fishing gear and walked down to the dock to his John boat.

He put the gear in the boat, turned and walked over to his minnow bucket partially submerged with live ones in it. He pulled it up and dangled it over the side of his boat in the water. He uses some different kinds of bates from time to time. He stepped in the boat and shoved off. The boat has an electric trolling motor and swivel seat up front to sit while using a foot peddle to operate the trolling motor.

He trolled out to the north side of the large dredged out thirty foot deep and two hundred foot square pond and cast his line over to the edge of the pond, sat back and relaxed. It wasn't a minute till he had a hit with a big channel cat. This cat feeds up in the water unlike the regular cats that feed off the bottom. The channel cat is a Florida game fish as such you can only catch so many.

The moon was about a half moon, so there wasn't that much light to see by. He wished it was a full moon so he could see better and the fish would bite better, also.

He then moved a little more toward the middle of the pond to go after the larger channel cats since they had moved into the pond from off Lake Tiger.

As he came around with the boat he thought he got a glimpse of something lying over on the small little island out from the south edge of the pond. It kind of shook him, causing him great fright. He became afraid to go any closer, but he did and wishes he hadn't later.

He told himself, don't be such a chicken. Go on over and investigate what it is you think you saw. As he slowly trolled over, closer and closer it became obvious it was a person. Ever so slowly he moved, nearer and nearer until...........yes it is a body of a woman. He could see the top of her head. She had blonde hair and was naked. One arm and one leg were dangling over the side of the island in the water. He could now see......... no, it can't be. The leg and arm had been gnawed off up to the knee and elbow.

He quickly turned the John boat around and headed for the dock. When he got it secured he took off like a rocket with those long legs just a pumping for the telephone to call 911.

Chapter

1

TIGER LAKE

My sidekick and friend from way back, Jerry Churchill, and I Rick Ulrick have lived here at Al's Ramp and Camp for several years now. Old Jerry is much of a man; he stands six one and weighs 220. He is big boned and hard as nails. Jerry can whip most men in a fair fight and is ready to fight most anytime. I feel good having him at my back. I'd take him over anybody else I know to back me up.

I, on the other hand, am six three and weigh in at 250. I'm big boned as well but not as quick tempered as Jerry. I won't take any trouble from anybody. I'd back Jerry to the death of me. We both feel the same way most of the time.

He has a nice motor home on a shady camp space right next to mine. I have a thirty-one-foot motor home with a queen-size bed, with plenty of room in it just like I like. My bathroom like in most motorhomes is small. It has a shower and tub it's too small for me, so I use the camp shower, vanity, and commode in it. The kitchen is small as well with a little, two-bench-seat dinette table that seats four. The living room has a couch and chair. It's just right for one person—me.

You see, Jerry doesn't have to worry about a thing because he retired early from the fire department and has a pension coming in from that, plus some income from rental houses in Tampa. He has a couple who look after the houses for him, so he doesn't have to work at anything if he doesn't want to. Each week I have a check coming in from the sale of my restaurant, so I don't have to work either if I don't want to.

I do love helping the police forces around the state that are understaffed and unable to solve some of their crimes. Its interesting work being a private investigator and solving some crimes that no one else has been able to solve, which I have done many times. I make a lot of money doing that and always share it with Jerry, since he is always helping me—and a big help he is.

I was married for a few years, but it didn't work out, and now I don't care if I ever marry again, as I like my single life. Jerry's life has been very much like mine, so much so that it's scary sometime to talk about it. We do meet some nice un-liberated women from time to time, like last year when two good lookers came cruising into camp in a big, new motor home the owner had when her husband died suddenly. They stayed for two weeks and left, but we had a good time with them the whole two weeks. I still stay in touch with the one I dated and liked.

I used to wake and fly-fish all the time, until I got surrounded by mother gators on the north side of the lake one spring time. They were hatching their young back in the grass line a ways. Usually they bed in a swampy area back from the waist-deep water's edge. I kept on fly-fishing, but I was watching the big, old, long, fat mama gator out in front of me and the boat. She was doing some funny things, trying to scare me away from her young ones.

Suddenly she slammed her tail down on the water so hard, it sounded like a shotgun going off. I'm telling you that scared me and showed me that she meant business. I turned and took a look back behind me and saw there was another one, plus another one out in the lake. They had me surrounded.

I pulled the rope hard and quick; I had tied the rope to my waist and to the boat. I got in and stayed in ever since. That cured me from wading, and I haven't waded since. I use my trolling motor now. You know, it's a funny thing about alligators; the mother will lay and then hatch as high as one hundred eggs. That means she has one hundred mouths to feed. Then one day at the first opportunity the male gator will eat as many as ninety or more of the baby gators.

Strange isn't it? I guess if it wasn't true, we would all be waist deep in alligators by now, huh?

It was a beautiful spring morning, just at the crack of dawn; the water was cool, fresh smelling with just a tiny bit of vapor coming off the water around the edge of the grass and reeds on Lake Tiger. As the lake cools at night after a hot daytime sun has heated it, vapor rises from the surface. The water hyacinths and other wild flowers along the bank smell so sweet. It was so quiet this early in the morning that the only sound I heard was an occasional bass jumping out of the water after a shiner. I could hear a Florida woodpecker off in the distance, pecking away. Florida woodpeckers are many times larger than the regular woodpecker we are used to, and his pecking is like a jackhammer—it's so loud. The grass and weed line was about thirty yards from shore and about belly high. It was just right for fly-fishing.

Lake Tiger is an elongated lake at about three miles long and a mile and a half wide, with Rosalie Creek running into it from Lake Rosalee on the north side and Tiger Creek running out of it into Lake Kissimmee on the east side. I have been fishing Lake Tiger and the Kissimmee chain of lakes for years now.

Jerry and I were out on the lake early before daybreak just when the big bass were moving in to feed. I had just caught a speckled perch (they are known as crappies in the north) on my fly rod with a small popper. They don't usually come to the top like that.

Only in the very early morning, and you never catch them on a fly rod. I did and do quite often. They are in the shallow waters around the grass, weeds, and reeds feeding on minnows before the heat of the day.

I was catching quite a few shell crackers, bluegill and bass on my fly rod this morning. I took them off the popper hook, opened the live well in front of my pedestal seat, and dropped them in. They were raising all kinds of fuss. Jumping out of the live well water and hitting the sides of the tank. It seemed like they would beat their brains out doing that if they didn't stop. Soon they did stop. They got tired, I guess. The live well has a pump that brings freshwater up out of the lake into it, and that keeps them alive much longer. The water also recirculates.

I pulled off some fly line and cast that fly line back and forth a time or two and laid it gently on the water right where I was looking. For years now I've been able to just look at where I want to cast, and that popper or fly will go right to that spot (just like the old gunfighters did back in the Wild West. They trained so much with a pistol, drawing it so fast, that they had no time to aim it. But they learned to look exactly where they wanted to hit and almost always hit what they looked at.). Then I twitched it a little and then gave it a little pop and BAM—a big bass hit it, and around and around we went.

I raised the rod tip to let it do the work and pulled in a little line. I worked him like that for a while, and soon he got tired, and that's when I brought him in. A bass of any size at all feels like a whale on a fly rod. I have two live wells in my bass boat, one in the front and one in the back. I had not heard Jerry catch a thing.

I looked back at Jerry in the back fishing chair, and he said, "Rick, if you will let me up there in that front chair, I will show you how to catch fish."

I laughed at him and told him, "You're not even trying"

"Ha," he said, "you know you can catch more fish from the front than you can from the back."

"You can cast in several directions, and I can only cast in one from up here. Besides, Jerry, it's my boat, and I get to sit anywhere I want."

"If you feel that way about it, I'll just stay home next time."

"Aw, don't be childish now. Get your popper in the water so you can catch something."

Soon he caught a nice bass, and that shut him up.

We went back in about ten o'clock before it got too hot. I could see there were quite a few people out on the lake now—some fishing around the shore like we like to do and some out in the middle in deeper water, drift-fishing for speckled perch. They are a fine eating fish.

I went real slow into the canal so as not to make any waves to disturb other boats and turned slowly into my slip. I stopped right over my cradle and stood up in the boat to reach the switch to turn on the winch to raise us up to dock level. We got our fish out of the deep well, stepped out on the dock, and took them up to the cleaning table, where we proceeded to clean our catch, which always draws a crowd.

Everybody wants to know all the particulars. Where, when, what, and how. Jerry and I always kept those details to ourselves, because we wanted to go back to that spot this evening and fish it some more. After cleaning and washing the fillets real good, we got out some quart-sized plastic bags to put them in and filled them up with water to freeze. It is said that fish frozen in water will last much, much longer than fish frozen without it.

We always have a mess of fish to eat. I always cut my bass fillets into fingers and dip them into this batter I make up before frying the fingers. They come out just as crisp as English fish and chips. Then I make up a good Miller High Life hush-puppy mix. Instead of water or milk, I poured in a can of Miller beer. Boy, are they good. I like cheese grits with my fish and sliced tomatoes and of course hush puppies. What a fine meal that is.

We used to hold back on our fish some, and pretty soon we would have a camp fish fry. Everybody in the camp was invited, whether he or she came or not. Al had a propane fryer that fried the heck out of fish. We dropped those bass fingers in that fryer, and they sank to the bottom. When they rose to the top, they were done. It took no time at all to cook up a batch of fish and hush puppies. We've had some great times

Chapter

2

SUN N' FUN CAMP FOR THE BLIND

Well, we are sitting around there at Al's Ramp and Camp after eating, talking about the next shoot over at Cape Canaveral. Wondering how many more we were going to shoot up before we run out of money.

About that time a sheriff's car drove up and stopped. It was old Sheriff Bill Dade of Polk County from over at Lake Wales. He got out of his car and shuffled over to us and took a seat. Bill looked a little scruffy to me. He is normally a very neat guy. Not all rumpled, wrinkled, and sweaty as he looks now. He looks like he's been through the mill and come out the looser.

I said, "What's the matter, Bill? Have they been running your legs off lately?"

"Ah, Rick, they just won't keep enough deputies to do the job, so it all falls back on me to do! Do you remember the other day? I told you I might be calling you. Well, here I am at your door."

I offered him a Miller, and he took it gladly, because this was a day for a cold one or two for sure.

Now, old Bill and I go way back. He and I have fished most of these lakes around here from time to time, and he is one of my favorite fishing partners. He's one of a few who beats me every once in a while. Bill has put on a few pounds around the middle and a little snow on top, but he is still much of a man.

"Rick, is your private investigator's license still in effect?"

"Jerry and I just got them renewed last month. I got some new business cards printed too. Here, have one or two. I renamed my business, Rick's Private Investigating Agency, Owner, Rick Ulrick, and Associate, Jerry Churchill. "

"Jerry whipped his out and showed it to him. I'm proud of this Bill and I'm looking forward to something new to do, so lay it on us."

"Good. I need your help on something, but the county can't pay you much. Fifty-eight thousand dollars plus expenses is it, but you have the experience to help us out, and we need help bad."

I thought to myself, If I can get several cases like this a year, I'll be sitting in high cotton.

"Bill, you know I would help you out for nothing."

"I know, Rick, but we all have to eat, and you need to make something so you can pay Jerry a little. He looks like he could use it."

"Sheriff Bill, it never ceases to amaze me how you can know me so well when you see me so seldom," Jerry said.

Bill laughed about that.

"Bill and Jerry, do you guys want another ice-cold bottle of Miller?"

Both said, "You bet, Rick."

I went into the motor home for three more cold ones out of the fridge, came back out, and handed one to each of them.

"Thanks, Rick," they both. They took a swallow and gave a big, "Ahhhh!"

Bill asked us if we knew what the Sun n' Fun Camp for the Blind was for and how it was funded. Its only function is to teach and help blind children how to get along in life and overcome their handicaps. It is a state-run and backed institution. I forget what the age range is for the children, but the staff does a great job with them. The camp is totally self-sustaining with all the facilities needed to do the job. It has two rows of little houses with two children paired up to each house. The houses face each other, with a little paved path down the middle and a handrail all along the way to a Y that splits off to the mess hall and ball field. The children and staff have their own kitchen, cooks, and dining hall. They use the dining hall for large gatherings and meetings. They have a great Olympic-size swimming pool and a nonalcoholic bar. There is a great boat ramp and canoes for the kids to use and about thirty camping spaces.

I said, "Okay, what's your trouble, Bill? Tell us what we are getting into."

"Someone found a body last night up at the Sun n' Fun Camp for the Blind. The caretaker, found her around midnight. He likes to go out catfish fishing at night. He's usually only fishing around inside the camp pond and catches all he wants right here.

He saw her in the moonlight out on that little man-made island that was dredged out of the pond at the camp. She was lying on her back naked with part of one leg and an arm chewed off by a gator. She had not been there too long, as rigor mortis had not set in. We don't know if she was placed on that island by the murderer or if a gator got her and drug her up onto it to finish eating her.

She appears to be somewhere in her late twenties, a very pretty blonde-headed woman. I got some strong lights and searched real well all over that island but found nothing. We took some good pictures of the island and the area where the body was lying. The medical examiner ran a Wood's Lamp all over the body, looking for traces of semen, but found none on her.

The body is at the Polk County morgue now. There was something like twenty RVs there at the camp for the Labor Day weekend. The kids were putting on a skit for their parents.

"Rick, have you ever gone over and watched how they work with those blind kids? It's awesome to see them play softball, swim, paddle a canoe, and do some of the other games they play. Take softball, for instant. They have a ball with holes in it that whistles while it goes through the air. The kids hear it and hit it with their bats, or catch it by sound. They whistle at each other so they will know where to throw the ball to.

"It's something to see. Rick, you might want to start over there at the camp, talking to some of the counselors to see what they might have seen, heard, or thinks."

"Okay, Bill. Old Jerry and I will crank up old Knock About and take a run over there this very afternoon."

Let me explain what the "Knock About" is. I had this Lincoln Town Car with eighteen thousand miles on it. I took it over to this friend of mine in town by the name of Sparks. He is the very best welder I have ever seen. I told him I wanted him to cut off the rear end of the Town Car behind the front seats down to the frame and put on a pickup truck body on the ass end of it. I wanted him to make me a Lincoln Town Car pickup truck. I went back in about a month, and he had me the most beautiful truck I have ever seen. He had painted it a creamy-gold color, with a beautiful clear-coat finish.

"Come look at it, Bill."

Bill walked around that truck and just shook his head. "That's the funniest-looking thing I ever seen. I guess if it works for you that are all that matters."

"It's the best darn riding truck you've ever rode in and a lot more handy than a Town Car too."

"You know that yesterday was a holiday, and there was lots of visitors at the camp all weekend. The lady that was killed was the wife of a Brandon attorney, Archie Crabtree, who was visiting their five-year-old blind son at the camp. The little boy's name is Albert. His mother's name was Linda Crabtree. Archie and Linda built a home on Hills Avenue there in Brandon. They both went to Brandon High School about the same time Toni Campbell and Donny Dempsey were going there. They both played football. Toni played tight end, and Donny played split end, and Denny Rawlinson was quarterback."

"Bill, the quarterback's father is a friend of mine. I know both Donny and Toni too."

"Do you know if Mr. Crabtree is still at the Sun n' Fun Camp? I'd like to talk to him if you think it's okay so soon after . . . you know."

"Yes, Rick, I think he is, because of his boy, Albert."

"Okay, Jerry and I are going over now. Are you driving, or do you want to ride with us?"

"No, Rick, I've got to go on back to Lake Wales."

"Let me know if you find out anything."

"Okay, sure will."

"Let's go, Jerry. I need to go out to Highway 60 to get some gas in old Knock About before we go anywhere."

Gus the funny owner was his usual jovial self, laughing and upbeat all the time. Gus is hard working and is usually covered in grease. Today he was neat as a pen. He must have a date after work to night.

He said, "Hey, boys. How's old Knock About doing? It's looking good to me."

"Yeah, Gus, it's the best car/truck I ever had," I said.

We filled her up, checked the oil, and drove on back north on Tiger Lake Road.

We passed Al's Ramp and Camp and went on to the Sun n' Fun Camp. We pulled into the visitor's parking space and parked. People gawked at old Knock About, probably wondering what it was. We headed for the camp office to see the superintendent. I knocked on the door and heard, "Come in."

We went in, introduced ourselves, and showed him our credentials. He said his name was Peter Peoples and asked what he could do for us. He was a fairly handsome fellow of about forty-five who wears no wedding ring. He was dressed in nice sports clothes, and his office was full of antiques and pictures of his family. He had lots of pictures of his mother and some of his father, brothers, and sister.

His desk and chair were something else again. You would never expect to see one like it way out here in a camp office. One might see one on Madison Avenue maybe but not here. It was a huge maple one polished to where you could see yourself in its surface, and his chair must have cost one thousand dollars alone. Did he really need to project that kind of image in this camp?

I said, "Did you know the deceased, Mr. Peoples?"

"No, I didn't know her, but I knew her husband and son."

"Did you do any socializing with them before Mrs. Crabtree's death?"

"No, I didn't!"

"What do you think happened to her?"

"I think she went down to the water's edge behind her motor home one time too many, and a gator got her. They seem to be losing their fear of man. Too much contact with humans."

Jerry said, "How well do you know the caretaker?"

"Not too well. He just started a month ago. He had good references, though."

"If you hear of anything we should know, call me at this number," I said, handing him my card. "We live down at Al's Ramp and Camp."

"Sure will, Rick."

"Is it okay if we talk to a few folks around here, like the caretaker?"

"Help yourself. After all, we are neighbors."

Jerry and I went looking for the caretaker to ask him some questions. Long John was clipping the shrubbery around some of the cabins and doing a super job of it to. We walked up to him, introduced ourselves, and showed him our credentials.

He said, "Howdy, I'm Long John Johnson."

"I understand you found that lady on the little island in the pond last night."

"Yep, I did, last night about midnight."

"Well, tell me about what you did last night from about six until you found the body."

"I had dinner in the dining hall at five thirty and then went back to my cabin to brush my teeth and clean up a bit. Then I went bed and took a nap. I got up, washed my face and hands, and changed into some old clothes to go catfish fishing. Went down to my johnboat, untied it and got in, trolled over to the middle of the dredged-out pond to fish. I looked over at the little man-made island and saw what looked like a body lying on it. It freaked me out at first, but I trolled on over to check anyway to see who or what it was. When I saw what it was, I trolled back in and reported it to nine one one and that was it."

"Did you know her before she died?"

"Only saw her a few times, but I didn't know her. No, I didn't know her, you know."

"You know, I was wondering. Did Mr. Peter Peoples know her very well?"

"He sure did. I used to see them together a lot. They—Mr. and Mrs. Crabtree and Mr. Peoples—went out to eat together a lot."

"Oh, yes, one more thing. Do you know Mr. Peoples very well?"

"I sure do. We have been inviting him to Ben and mines poker games quite a few times."

"What do you think of him?"

"He is a stinking cheat. He deals from the bottom of the deck and is real slick at it too, but I caught him at it several times. But I didn't say anything because he's my boss."

I handed him my business card and asked him to call me if anything turned up he thought we needed to know. He said he would.

Chapter

3

IT'S SLOW GOING

*J*erry said, "Rick I wonder why Peter Peoples lied so much to us. Is he trying to cover up something or what? He could have been sneaking over to visit Linda Crabtree at night every time Archie went back to Brandon for some business reasons. He could have killed her last night and laid her body out on the little island behind her motor home to make it look like Archie did it."

"I just don't know, Jerry. I just don't know."

We went over behind the swimming pool to where the RVs were parked to look up Mr. Crabtree and ask him a few questions. We rounded the corner of the pool house, and there he sat under the awning of his motor home, drinking a cold Miller High Life. We walked up to him, and he looked up at us and said, "Hi, fellows, I'm Archie Crabtree, want a beer?"

I took one look at the sweat running down the side of that bottle and said, "You bet your sweet potato I do. That's my favorite beer you're drinking. Jerry will have one too I'll bet."

He went inside and got us one each. He had already opened them for us. I took a long swallow, and it tasted like heaven to me. What a great beer!

"What can I do for you fellows?"

"I'm Rick Ulrick and this is my side-kick, best friend, and fishing partner, Jerry Churchill. We are private investigators working for Polk County and Sherriff Bill Dade, investigating your wife's death"

"Glad to meet you. I'm the husband of the deceased."

"Pleasure meeting you," I said.

I could tell he had had several of these beers before we got here because he looked like he was feeling no pain.

"Mr. Crabtree, I would like to know where you were last night when your wife was found around midnight."

"I had just gotten back from Lake Wales when I heard the commotion and saw the crowd out back of my motor home."

"What did you do in Lake Wales?" Jerry asked.

"I went to a movie and then came straight home."

"Then what did you do?"

"I went over to the pond to see what the commotion was all about. Someone saw me and said they had found my wife lying dead on that little island in the pond. I freaked out then. The police wanted to talk to me, but I was in no shape to do so. The doctor gave me something that knocked me out for hours. So here we are talking about it today."

"Had you and your wife been having any marital problems, like being unfaithful to each other, et cetera?"

"We did a couple of times. It was mostly me and my jealousy. You see, guys were always hitting on her in my presence, and it made me terribly jealous."

"Is there anyone you know of that might have done this to her?"

"No, I don't. Sorry!"

"Okay, Archie, if you remember anything that might help us, please call me at this number, and thanks for the beer. Oh, by the way, I meant to ask you where you were from before Florida."

"I'm from Greenville, South Carolina."

"That's my home town," I told him. "It's a small world, isn't it? So long Archie. We will be seeing you again soon."

We went over to the pond to look at the island. It is just a very small man-made island with grass and weeds growing on it and no trees, mainly because it's not big enough for trees.

"Jerry, let's you and I get down on our knees and search the grass by spreading it with our fingers to see what we can find, if anything," I said. "You take the left side, and I'll take the right side, then we will meet and come back down the middle. Okay with you? Then we won't have to wonder. We will know that nothing is there hidden in the grass and weeds."

We walked over to each side and started looking. Jerry had not crawled very far when he said, "Well, look at this, will you?" Jerry sat up while holding up what looked like a black ball-point pen.

I asked, "Is there anything written on it?"

"Yes. There is. It says, 'Archie Crabtree Esquire, Attorney at law, 114 Oakfield Drive, Brandon, Florida, 33511.' Well, what do you think about this?"

"It's maybe more frame-up, huh? Somebody could have tossed it over here from over at his motor home."

"Can you believe it, Jerry—Archie being from Greenville? That's good, though, because I can get my longtime friend, Barry, to find out all he can about Archie. Barry will find out a lot about our Mr. Archie Crabtree. You just wait and see. I'm sure he still has his PI license in effect."

"Listen, Rick. I have a funny feeling about this murder. Do you feel like he did this thing himself? I don't because I haven't ever met a lawyer dumb enough to murder his wife and take her outside, behind his motor home, and lay her on an island for everybody to see, and not expect them to think it was him that did it. It's just too much that doesn't make sense about all this. I think somebody is trying to lay it on him to make him look guilty."

As we walked around the side of the motorhome, Archie's bass boat and trailer was sitting there and I noticed some kind of weed hanging down from the axel of the trailer. I reached down and picked it off and stuffed it down into one of my pockets. I told Jerry I would put it into a Ziploc bag and put it in the freezer to preserve it.

It was getting on toward dinnertime, and I was hungry. I asked Jerry if he was hungry.

He said, "Hungry as a bear."

"Let's go down to Mama Bell's Country Kitchen on Highway 60."

I said, "Sounds good to me. Let's do that." And away we went in the Knock About.

Now Mama Bell's is a restaurant that serves up some of the very best food this side of heaven. If it hadn't been for Mama Bell, Jerry and I would have starved to death long time ago. Mama Bell can cook vegetables like my mama used to do. She seasons them and cooks them until they are done just right. Oh, what heavenly food.

I feel so sorry for the other restaurants in Lake Wales that will never catch on to her seasoning and cooking. Why, every time I walk into Mama Bell's, I feel like I just got home again. Mama Bell's barbecue beef ribs are a sin. I don't know how she cooks them, but when they get to my plate, they are the best things I ever tasted. She cooks them until the meat just about falls off the bone, with a little Sweet Baby Ray's BBQ Sauce. Boy, they are lip-smacking good.

Old Jerry and I ordered some of them, and I ordered some fried okra, fried until it's crunchy;

some stewed summer squash and onions; and some of Mama's corn bread. It's corn bread to die for, I'm telling you! It's not that sweet stuff you get at most places. And then the biggest and best glass of iced tea there ever was. Last, but not least, a helping of Mama's blackberry cobbler pie. Berries handpicked and delivered this morning, and pies made and baked by none other than Mama Bell herself. Oh, Lord helps me. I've done it again.

We paid and thanked Mama Bell, giving her a big tip and a hug. I told her we couldn't wait to get back to see her and eat some more of her food. She just grinned and loved it.

I drove us on back to our motor homes for some shut-eye.

I said to Jerry, "let's go back over to the Fun n' Sun Camp in the morning and talk to some of the kids to see if they have any ideas that might help us."

Jerry said, "Wake me when you get up, okay?"

I said, "Okay I will."

Jerry just hates an alarm clock of any kind. He likes to sleep until he gets enough, and then wake up. It's good for him, he says. I went into my motor home, washed up, brushed my teeth, and went straight to bed and fell into a deep sleep.

Chapter

4

SEARCHING FOR CLUES

I woke up around seven o'clock and made some coffee. Shaved and washed up and dressed while it perked. I poured two cups of coffee and went over to Jerry's motor home, opened the door, quietly walked to his bed, and waved that coffee cup under his nose. He sniffed and sat straight up in bed.

He said, "What are you doing, Rick?"

"I brought you a cup of mud to wake you up, old man."

"Give me a minute, and I'll be right with you."

I stepped outside and sat in one of his chairs under his awning, drank my coffee, and waited on him. He was just a minute or two. Then he came out and sat to drink his coffee too.

I asked, "Jerry, are you hungry?" He gave me his standard answer.

"I'm hungry as a bear."

"Let's go down to Mama Bell's to get her world's best breakfast." And off we went in the old Knock About.

It only takes us about eight minutes to get there, as it's only about three or four miles down there. We both ordered the Champion Breakfast. It consists of country-cured ham, sausage (with sage) or bacon, two eggs, cheese grits, sliced tomatoes, and some of Mama's award-winning biscuits with sausage gravy on the side. Man, you can plow a field with that breakfast. I can only eat it about once a week. Jerry left a tip, and we left.

I drove us back up to the camp for the blind and pulled into a space to go see the kids. They had just finished their breakfast and were already out playing ball and doing other activities. We went into the dining hall, and there were a few who hadn't finished yet. One pretty, little blonde lady was sitting by herself, so we went over to her and introduced ourselves. We told her we were working with the sheriff on the case of Mrs. Archie Crabtree. She said that her name was Becky Lake and that she was blind and was there for the summer to learn how to do a lot of new things, she says, "to help me out in life." I asked her if I could ask her some questions about Mrs. Crabtree.

She said, "Yes that will be fine. Go right ahead."

"Did you know the deceased, Linda Crabtree?"

"Yes, very well. I'm a friend of their son, Alfred, and I sleep over at their house sometimes to take care of him. We play games for the blind, laugh, and have lots of fun. Mrs. Crabtree has always been nice to me. She would make us cookies and cakes, et cetera. Let us play in the pool while supervising us.

"She seemed to be just fine to me. She did drink too much sometimes to be a good mother. I thought she should have been more attentive to Alfred. She just let him do as he pleased, almost all the time."

"Did Mr. and Mrs. Crabtree ever have fights while you were visiting them?"

"Sometimes they did. Truthfully I don't think they loved each other very much."

"What did they fight about, as far as you could tell?"

"It was mostly his jealousy of her."

"Did she ever do things that caused him to be Jealous?"

"She would talk about other men when he was around to hear it. Once or twice other men dropped by and paid a little too much attention to her, I guess."

"Becky, do you have any idea who might have done this to her?"

"No, I don't. I have my suspicions, but I'll let you know who when I definitely know."

"If you remember or hear of anything else that you think we should know, please call us at this number on my card."

"I sure will, Mr. Ulrick."

As we were leaving the dining hall, we heard some of the kids out in Lake Tiger. They were in a canoe, laughing and paddling away. A counselor was in the boat, coaching them and telling them which way to go, and what to do.

We left the dining hall, and went over toward the boat ramp, where we saw Long John cleaning out his johnboat. He saw us and waved us over. We walked on over, and I asked, "How's it going, Long John?"

He said, "You know, guys, I was thinking about what we talked about last time you were here and remembered hearing what sounded like a boat out on the lake the night I found that lady's body. I have never heard anybody else out on the lake around midnight when I usually go out. I thought that was unusual, so I thought I would tell you about it."

Rick said, "Thanks, Long John. That might come in handy."

After we left him, Jerry said to me, "You don't think he was just telling us that, about hearing a boat on the lake, to take our mind off of him, do you?"

I said, "Time will tell, Jerry. Time will tell."

We walked over and watched the kids play softball a while. They were really into it and enjoyed it very much. You could tell by their excited, sweaty, and smiling faces that they loved it. It was surprising to us how many hit that ball that was pitched to them. It was interesting too how they whistled to each other to let each other know where to throw the ball. Also amazing, was how the ball whistles on its way to let the one trying to catch it know where it is. The kids laughed a lot, so we knew they were enjoying themselves.

It was getting on toward noontime. Jerry suggested we go back to our motor homes, deep-fry us some bass fillets, and make us some fish sandwiches for lunch.

I said, "Okay," and drove on down Tiger Lake Road to Paul's Road. I turned left and drove about a mile down to Al's Ramp and Camp.

I fixed up the condiments for the sandwiches, while Jerry fried the fillets.

"Want a cold beer, Jerry?"

He laughed and said, "You bet I do Rick."

I sliced up a ripe tomato, sliced a Vidalia onion, pulled off some lettuce leaves, then got out the tartar sauce and hamburgers buns. I toasted the buns in the toaster oven.

We ate our fill of fish sandwiches and beer, and got sleepy. Jerry went into his motor home, and I went into mine, and we took a two-hour nap. I woke up at two thirty and felt rested, so I went to Jerry's, woke him up, and asked him if he wanted to ride with me into Lake Wales.

He said, "Give me a minute."

"Come on over when you get ready."

In a little bit he came around the front of my motor home with a smile on his face and decked out for something other than what I had in mind.

He had shaved, and boy did his after shave smell.

"Jerry, what is that stuff you have on?"

"It's that aftershave you gave me last Christmas."

"Whew, that stuff is strong. It's one Bonnie gave me that I didn't like, but I thought maybe you just might like it. I had forgotten how it smelled."

"Well, thanks a lot partner for that big favor. Just don't do me anymore favors like that one, please! Why you would think I was your enemy instead of your friend and partner."

We got in the Knock About, and I drove us to Lake Wales. I told Jerry I thought we should go to the morgue to view the body and talk to the medical examiner about what progress he had made. I drove downtown and passed the Florida Hotel almost to the Negro quarters, where the morgue was. We went in, and there was Dr. Jack Cutlet, the

ME on duty. I told him I wanted to see Linda Crabtree's body if he didn't mind.

He said, "Okay, Rick, just a minute."

He rolled her out of cold storage on a gurney, pushed her into the autopsy room, and uncovered her. What a mess she was in. He had finished the autopsy on her, and the body looked ghastly. She was missing most of her left arm and half of her left leg, and of course Jack had cut her from throat to groin. The left side of her head and face looked like the gator had gnawed on them. She was one hideous sight. Evidently her left leg and arm had dangled in the water while she was lying on the island. She had scratches on several other parts of her body as if the gator had pawed at her. She was a natural blonde and had been very pretty.

"Jack, what did you decide was the cause of death?" I asked.

"The gator didn't kill her or drown her. He didn't even drag her off the island. He just lay there, eating her at his leisure. The caretaker must have scared him off when he found her."

"Well, what did she die of?"

"As far as I can tell, she died of a blow to the left temple by what looks like a big ring. Under microscopic examination I can just make out a design of some kind that would be on a ring."

"Is that right? Something like a college ring, maybe?"

"Yes, that's it exactly—or bigger."

"I don't think I remember seeing one that big on anyone's finger around here yet, Jack. Have you seen one on anyone, Jerry?"

"Rick, it doesn't take much of a blow to the temple to kill someone. I can remember when I was a kid. The next-door neighbor's boys were playing with each other one evening after school, and one threw a marble at the other; hit him in the temple and he hit the ground. It just knocked him out, but it could have killed him. You see, in this case she was already dead when the gator was doing his dirty work on her."

"Can you keep that about the ring from the public for a while? I need some time."

"Yes I can and will, but let me know when I can release it, please."

"Thanks, Jack you've been a great help to us and we appreciate it."

"Think nothing of it, it's my job you know, and besides I like you and Jerry."

When we got back into the Knock About, Jerry didn't smell the same as he had before we went into the morgue.

I asked Jerry if he wanted some of Bare Bones Bar-B-Que. Their baby back ribs are the best. The meat just falls off the bone, and I had a hunger for some of those and some of their sweet corn on the cob.

Jerry said, "I don't believe I do, Rick." So we headed on back to the camp.

When we arrived back at Al's Ramp and Camp, several fishermen were down at the dock cleaning fish and telling lies. We walked down to see how they were biting. Old Sniffy was there with a pair of bass I could hardly believe.

"Wow, where did you get them, Sniffy?" I asked.

"In Lake Kissimmee," he said.

"Boy, I'll bet they were fun to catch."

He said, "No sir, they hardly fought at all. They are too big to fight, I figure."

"I'm going to mount this biggest one here," he said, holding up the biggest one for me to see.

"What did he weigh, Sniffy?"

"He weighed twelve pounds, six ounces."

"Nice," I said.

Sniffy got his nickname from a habit he has of always sniffing, honking, rubbing, and blowing his nose.

I walked on down to my bass boat to check on it. It was just fine. I hoped we could wrap up this case soon so we could get back out there and catch us some of those whoppers. We went on back up to the motor homes and went to bed. I was tired.

"Jerry," I said the next morning, "I think we need to take a trip into Brandon to see if we can pick up anything about this case to help us. We can pay a visit to Mr. Crabtree's office and talk to some of his employees and go by his home to maybe talk to some of his neighbors. We need to see just what people think of him."

Jerry said, "That's okay with me. When do you want to leave?"

"Is right now fin with you?"

"Let me get a few things for the road."

I went into the motor home to get some meds I take, my shaving kit and a change of clothes, then came on out. Jerry was ready. We took off in old Knock About after locking up. We used too, never lock anything. Now, with all the dope heads around the country they might steal your motor home and boat if they want them bad enough. I personally think dope causes most of our crime today. The dope heads come down off a high and need more, so what is the first thing they think of? Steal something to sell, to get more.

It was a typical central Florida morning, cool and fresh smelling. It was a great-to-be-alive morning. Rain water stood in the ditches along both sides of Highway 60 from the showers over the last several days. Every once in a while, if you look close, you can see small gators in them if you're lucky. *I love Florida.* What a great state.

As we traveled along Highway 60, I asked Jerry what he thought about stopping at Mama Bell's to get her to fix us some of her good sausage and biscuits and two cups of hot coffee to go. All he said was "Yummy!" I pulled in at Mama Bell's, and we went in to find Mama Bell her usual bright and smiling self. We hugged her and placed our order.

She got our coffee, and we sat there, blowing and sipping.

Mama Bell is about forty five years old, and tends to stay on the chubby side. She moved into this building and has made it a land mark place to eat. She had a great cook for a mother and she taught her how to put the grub together in a wonderful fashion. She always has on a clean apron, keeps herself looking good and evidently is a great trainer and manager. She does a great job at PR work, I know that.

Soon we had our order and a coffee refill, and told Mama Bell bye and left for Brandon. We were on our way, eating hot sausage and biscuits. Mama Bell puts quite a bit of sage in her sausage, just the way I like it, and her biscuits are thin and light, brown and crunchy, when you bite into them. Boy, are they good. They are not those big, fat doughy ones you get at most places. I won't eat them unless I can open the biscuits, reach in, and pull out the big wad of dough most have in them. I alter them to suit me.

Chapter

5

THE BRANDON VISIT

efore I knew it, we were in Bartow, the county seat of Polk County. We were driving through Mulberry and on the way to Brandon. I met this guy over at the fish camp one time from Clearwater, who told me about this little old place called Campbell's Dairyland that had the best chili dogs anywhere. He said he lived in Clearwater and worked in Mulberry. He made that trip both ways each day. He said a guy from Brandon who worked with him told him about Campbell's and their chili dogs, so I stopped one time to check them out.

I found out they have a foot long that is just right for my taste. I soon started stopping several times a week to get me two foot longs to take home for dinner for me and my wife. A guy who worked at Campbell's asked me how far I hauled my chili dogs, because they tend to get a little soggy after a while, and I said, Clearwater. But, you see, I was traveling into the evening sun, so I laid them on my dash for the sun to keep them warm until I got home. I would rather have them that way than no way at all. Boy, I had to try them! Soon I was stopping right regular-like.

Brandon is a nice little town of about 120,000 souls. It is six miles east of Tampa out Highway 60. It is a bedroom community of Tampa.

Soon we were in Brandon, so I took a left off Highway 60 onto Parsons Avenue and drove one block. We pulled into the drive-thru of Campbell's Dairyland, the best, little ice cream and sandwich shop anywhere around. We both ordered a medium-size yogurt cone dipped in chocolate-cone dip from a lady named Jill. We asked where Mr. Crabtree's office was, and a guy named Jay came to the window and said it was west of Kings Avenue out Oakfield Drive on the right where Tampa Bay Federal is. He and Jill were pleasant, friendly folks.

We thanked him and pulled off, and he gave old Knock About a stare as if to say, *what is that?* We went looking and a licking. We finished our cones and went into the building where Archie's office is. We walked up to the receptionist, who was a very attractive brunette with a tight sweater, and introduced ourselves. We showed her our credentials, told her we were working for the sheriff of Polk County, and asked if Mr. Crabtree was in.

She said he wasn't, but she would have him call me if I left my number. "But," she said, "I really hate to call him at time like this."

I said, "Don't, and I'll understand. We would like to ask you a few questions, if you don't mind, please."

"What do you want to know?" She said.

"We are wondering if Mr. and Mrs. Crabtree were faithful to each other, that you know of."

"As far as I know, they were, but she was always making him jealous of her in many ways. Flirting with men mostly, and the way she acted around them, laughing and touching them. She drove Mr. Crabtree crazy sometimes. I only saw Mr. Crabtree get all flustered over a female client one time, but she was a blonde-headed knock out. For some unknown reason, he prefers blonde women. It makes me wonder why he hired me."

"Has he ever made a pass at you?" Jerry asked."

"No, he hasn't."

"What do you think of him?"

"He is a good lawyer, employer, and a likeable man but a little disturbed sometimes in a funny sort of way."

"Do you know anyone who might have done this to Mrs. Crabtree?"

"No, I don't."

"Thank you for your cooperation," I said, and if you think of anything later you think we should know, please call me at this number." I handed her my card.

"You're welcome, and I sure will."

"Bye now."

I looked up Hills Avenue on my GPS, and we headed that way, back to Kings Avenue. The GPS took us right to Hills Avenue. We turned left and went about a block, and there it was at the end of the street: a very impressive three-story old brick house with leaded windows and a beautifully landscaped lot.

Jerry took the right side of the street, and I took the left. The plan was to canvas as many neighbors as possible for the rest of the morning. At Rick's first house, the owners were at work, but the maid was home. She is a middle age black woman with greying hair. She was neatly dressed and spoke well and clearly. She told me her name is Jennie Mae. I introduced myself, gave her my card, and told her I was working the Crabtree case from over at Lake Tiger.

"May I ask you a few questions?" I asked.

She said, "Sure, come on in and fire away. She led the way into a sitting room off to the left of the foyer."

"First, did you know Mrs. Crabtree met with an accident that took her life?" I asked.

"Yes, I know about it. I know their maid very well, and she told me all about it. She is my sister-in-law."

"What is your sister-in-law's name?" Jennie Mae

"Her name is Emma Lou Haskins."

"Tell me in your own words what Emma Lou said about it all, Jennie Mae."

"Emma Lou went to work for the Crabtree's about four years ago. She thought at first it was going to be a soft, quiet job, but the Mrs. kept her jumping all the time."

"Where is she from?"

"She's from Greenville, South Carolina. Her mother still lives there. She was named after her grandmother, whose name was Emma Lou Harris."

"You've got to be kidding me!" I said.

"Emma Lou Harris took care of me when my mama was weaving at Judson Mill from the time I was two until I was seven."

"My goodness, Emma says, while shaking her head, what a small world it is. You are from Greenville too? My, my, what do you know about that?"

"Yes I am, I lived there until I was about eighteen years old."

I said, "Now tell me what she told you."

"She said the Crabtree's were not too easy to work for. She said the Mrs. was hell on wheels. The Mr. was not too bad and must make plenty of money. She was all the time making real expensive purchases of things, and he was forever giving her down the road about them. They have the very best of everything—appliances, cars, furniture, clothes, et cetera. She liked the men though. He was mad all the time about that. He was real suspicious of her.

"Oh, I'm sorry, where's my manners today. Would you like some refreshment, maybe a glass of lemonade, or some ice tea?"

"Some lemonade if you have some already made."

"I sure do, coming right up. Would you like some fresh baked oatmeal cookies to go with that lemonade?"

"No thank you. Then I asked her to tell me what she knows about the Crabtree's."

"She remembered one time Mr. Crabtree had to go out of town on a case he was working on. While he was gone, the Mrs. had a pool party and invited some of her friends. Some of her friends invited people too. Especially some single people, men and women. She had me fix up some fancy food stuff and order plenty of booze and beer."

Emma Lou continued saying, "The Mrs. wore a very tight and tiny bikini that night. All the men were gawking at her with desire in their eyes. There must have been fifty people showed up at that party I declare that woman is hell on wheels!"

The Mrs. was drinking heavy and got a little drunk, so she went upstairs to freshen up and never came back down again. She thinks one of the single guys had sneaked upstairs while nobody was looking and stayed with her all night long. She said this kind of stuff went on all the time."

"I thanked her for the refreshments and the information and gave her my card."

I went on to the next two homes. No one was home in the first one, but the lady of the house was home in the last one. I knocked, she came to the door, and I explained who I was and said that I wanted to ask her a few questions. I showed her my credentials.

She nodded her head and said, "Sure, have a seat." She indicated one of the chairs on the porch.

I asked her how well she knew Mr. and Mrs. Crabtree.

"She and I went to US Fitness on the same mornings and went out to lunch at Campbell's Dairyland a few times. That's my favorite place to get a bite or have some ice cream. My husband just loves their chili dogs. They have the best salads of any place anywhere. They give you your money's worth too.

"Linda Crabtree was a first-class flirt. She thought she was God's gift to men. She got downright disgusting with it sometimes. She embarrassed me. This is the only social-izing I did with her, and I know firsthand very little about her, but I have heard many stories about her, and none are good."

I thanked her and left to hunt down Jerry. He was sitting in the car, waiting on me.

He said he found only one person home, and she said that the Crabtree's were planning on getting a divorce, or so she heard. Mrs. Crabtree has said, the Mr. was holding it up because she was trying to take him to the cleaners.

I asked him if he wanted to go for lunch, and he said, "You bet your sweet patotie I do."

"I know, I know!"

I went back down to Parson's Avenue and turned into Campbell's. We went in, and a girl named Leesa waited on us. She looked like she was Korean with a Jewish nose. She was very nice with a pretty smile, which she used generously while waiting on us.

She gave us a pass-out menu even though they had a large menu up behind the counter. The pass-out menu has all the ingredients listed on it. We sat down to look it over. The Caribbean salad looked and read like it was a winner. Jerry liked the sound of the taco salad. So we ordered two ice teas and both the taco and Caribbean salads. Leesa gave us our ice teas,

She said, "We will call you when your food is ready. You may sit inside or outside; you will hear us call you either way,."

After a bit, I heard them call, "Rick, your food order is ready," so I went in and got it. They served it on a tray. I took it back outside to sit at one of the nice tables under the roof, with fans hanging down and cooling us off.

My Caribbean salad was in a deep-fried tortilla shell bowl you could eat as you ate your salad. They call it the "Incredible Edible Bowl." The salad had chopped lettuce, a scoop of potato salad, finely diced onions, chopped tomatoes, grated cheddar, chopped lettuce and chopped breast of fried chicken, slivered toasted almonds, sweet shredded coconut, and diced pineapple, with honey mustard dressing.

Jerry's taco salad was also in a tortilla shell and had chopped lettuce, diced tomatoes, sour cream, diced onions, some of Campbell's famous chili, shredded cheese, sliced black olives and taco sauce. That was, without a doubt, the very best salad I've ever had, and it was reasonably priced too. I went in and got us a couple of frozen cherry cheesecakes on a stick dipped in chocolate, said good bye to Leesa, and headed back to the camp.

Chapter

6

BACK TRACKING

I turned right off Parsons Avenue onto Highway 60 and headed toward home. I stopped at a produce stand on the edge of a strawberry field and bought a flat of strawberries for us to take home. I gave Jerry half of them. I like to cut them up over cereal in the morning. We made good time as it was before all the traffic from the mines let out. I stopped at the Wal-Mart just the other side of Bartow and bought some fill-in groceries and stuff. We got home about dinner time, but neither of us was hungry, so we went down to the docks to see who was there.

It seemed that while we were gone this guy had shot a gator that had come into the canal where we keep out boats. Some lady who doesn't like anyone shooting in the park called the game warden and told him that this guy had shot a gator. You see, it's against the law to shoot them. Well, the game warden came a running at that, all excited, looking for somebody to arrest for shooting an alligator.

I knew the man who shot the gator and told him we better get rid of it before the warden got here. So we went out in his boat, since it was already in the water. We found the gator and took him off quite a ways down to the right shore to hide him up in the weeds along the shore.

The game wardens can't prove anything without a carcass. They looked and looked for the gator in their boat but could never find it. They came back and accused just about all of us of having its tail in our freezers in our homes. The tail is the only part you eat off a gator. Restaurants here in Florida serve fried Alligator tail. They wanted to search our motor homes, but we told them we weren't here when the shooting happened, so they didn't search ours. They finally left mad as wet hens. I found out that the man who shot the gator had its tail in his freezer. Boy, what a gutsy fellow he was, because the wardens can take your car, boat, motor home, or trailer if they want to.

We went on up to our motor homes, and I put away what groceries I had purchased and went to bed. I was dog tired. The next morning I had me a bowl of cereal—honey-coated puffed wheat and Cheerios mixed together in a bowl of milk—and sliced strawberries for breakfast. When I was finished, I washed out the bowl, spoon, and knife, and laid them on a towel to dry. Rinsed out my coffee cup and laid it upside down to dry also. Now they are ready for in the morning. I find, doing it that way I never have a sink full of dishes. It is so easy to keep things neat when you live alone.

I took out of the freezer the weed I had taken off Mr. Crabtree's boat trailer; I had frozen it in a Ziploc bag. I asked Jerry if he wanted to go with me down to Camp Fins to talk to Clyde Lewis. He said he had a head-ache and was staying in bed.

I said, "Okay, hope you get to feeling better soon, and left for Camp Fins."

I went down Tiger Lake Road to Highway 60, turned left, and went to Lake Road and Camp Fins. Betty, Clyde's wife, was running things, and Clyde was taking it easy, recovering from a heart attack. He was resting under a shade tree, so I walked over to talk to him.

I showed him the Ziploc bag with the weed in it and asked him if he had ever seen anything like it before; he said I could find all I wanted near the ramp and along each side of the canal.

He was watching these two boys with pit bulls launch their airboats. One of the guys had the pit bulls up on the boardwalk and was teaching them to dive in the water after a stick. They were fearless. The guys finally left in their airboats and good riddance as far as I'm concerned, because I hate the darn things. I then walked over to hunt for a piece of the weed I was looking for, and sure enough, there was plenty of it.

Clyde said, "The Florida wildlife sprayers try to keep it killed back, but it keeps hanging around."

I asked old Clyde how he was doing, and he said, "Not too good, Rick. I just keep having bad health for some reason. Betty is working herself to death too. We want to sell out. You want to buy the camp, Rick?"

"No thank you! I'm working on the case of the death of the young woman over at the Sun n' Fun Camp."

"Yes, I heard about that the other day. Terrible thing, wasn't it? How was she killed, Rick? Was she shot or drowned? We haven't had any killing around here in many years. Are you making any progress?"

"We know how she died, but we can't talk about it yet. I'm checking every lead, trying to come up with something that will tell us who it might have been. I found this weed hanging off the woman's husband Archie Crabtree's boat trailer axle."

"He comes down here every once in a while to put in for some reason. It's puzzling to me when he could put in right there at the Blind Camp for nothing."

"Well, thanks Clyde, and if you hear of anything, give me a call on this number here on my card."

"I sure will, Rick."

When I got back to Al's Ramp and Camp, Jerry was feeling a little better.

I told him I had found the weed down at Camp Fins.

"Archie has been going down there every once in a while, putting in his boat for some reason. He has to pay there when he could launch from the Blind Camp for free. Puzzling, isn't it?"

I held up the two Ziploc bags with the weeds in them for Jerry to see, they were the same.

"We will need to pay Mr. Archie Crabtree another visit soon, very soon. Come on over to my place, and let's have us a cold one and talk a while."

He said, "Okay!"

Chapter

7

WHAT DO WE HAVE
SO FAR?

*J*erry came over in a bit, and we sat outside under the awning, drinking Miller High Life and just plain relaxing. It was another fine Florida day, sunshiny with a slight breeze blowing through the Florida oaks, swaying the Spanish moss to and fro. There were bald eagles and hawks screeching in the sky, and squirrels chattering on the ground and in the oaks. They came around looking for a handout, thinking we were eating something. Panhandlers, they are. The eagles were almost existent for a few years. We see some eagles every time we go fishing now.

It was about 79 degrees and low humidity. It was perfect weather for snowbirds to come to Florida. They would be flocking north soon. In mid-March or early April, the relentless Florida sun nudges up the temperature in a farewell salute to the snowbirds, who with their RVs and trailers exit the state via I-95, I-75, I-10, and other highways in a procession not unlike the wagon trains of old.

Their idealistic, low-stress pursuit of balmy weather and the good life is ongoing as they head back to their homes in Canada, Ohio, Georgia, Michigan, Pennsylvania, Indiana, Alabama, New York, and other states across the country. In place of long, dreary winters, slippery roads, and the dreaded snow shovel, they are enjoying scurrying sandpipers, and snoozing on the beach, early-morning golf, lingering lunches with fellow snowbirds, the sights of Florida, and best of all, a sense of freedom.

Roy and Joyce Cooper from Louisville, Kentucky, winter at Al's Ramp and Camp from November to Easter, our snowbird time. After Easter it's like someone said, "Evacuate." It costs us only $400 a month for a site for our motor home and that includes, power, water, and sewer.

Many snowbirds who are burned out on Florida's commercial attractions have found the state is filled with nature and natural phenomenon as seen in the state parks. This is the side of the state most tourists don't get to see; it's the part I love.

Chapter

8

WE ARE FINDING OUT MORE ABOUT MR. PEOPLES

*H*ere, Jerry, have an ice-cold Miller."

"I believe I will, Rick."

"Well, let's see what we have, and what do we think about this murder? We went to see and talked to handsome and single Peter Peoples, and he said he didn't know Mrs. Crabtree at all, yet when we talked to Long John, he said that he knew her very well. I wonder why Mr. Peoples told us that.

I started to take another sip of my beer and...........splat, a big gob of crane poop hit right on the top. Then we heard this awful racket in the air over our heads. It was a flock of Florida Cranes flying overhead making their loud calls. Man what a racket they make. I got up, threw the dirty beer in the trash and got me another one.

The thing about Mr. Peoples cheating at poker doesn't sound too good either. Also, I've been wondering why Long John told us about hearing a boat out on the lake at midnight about the time he found the body, when he never ever hears one that late on the lake. Then we have Mr. Crabtree going to a movie in Lake Wales by himself, when Mrs. Crabtree is there with him at the camp.

Strange! Plus, there's all her drinking and playing around with other men. It's got my head spinning round and round. I don't know what to think. We have to find out, though. Let's go talk to Al about some of this stuff, Jerry. What do you say?"

"Sure, let's go."

We went down to the docks, looking for Al. He was down there in the air-conditioned office doing some paperwork.

Al and his wife Lana bought the camp from a widow whose husband built it and then died leaving it to her to run. It was too much for her alone, so she sold it to Al. Al is as bald as a cue ball, but is a nice looking man otherwise. He is loaded with dough and has been buying land around the lake for a while now. He is tough as shoe leather and when he gets his dander up, mean as a snake. He will not take any thing off anybody, ever. It's all Lana can do to keep Al under control sometimes, but she manages somehow.

I said, "Al, can we talk to you a bit?"

"Sure," he said, laying his paper and pen down.

"I need to ask you what you know about the dead lady over at the Blind Camp."

"I probably don't know any more than you do, Rick."

"We talked to Mr. Peoples yesterday and found out a little bit. He lies, for one thing. He's dishonest for another."

"See, I knew you knew more than me. He is a lying son of a gun, for sure. He said he would chip in some when we were soliciting funds to make some improvements around the lake one time. He never kicked in a copper penny. Another thing that hacks me off is this; you know they like to take the kids fishing, and they just love it. He expects me to supply him with worms, minnows, and shiners for them to use, never thinking that I have to buy them just like he should be doing. I'm not here for my health, you know. A man has to make money to keep the place open. I won't do it, I tell you. Let him purchase his own bait, I say. I guess he is used to people donating stuff to his cause or something.

"One time he came down to one of our fish fries we had out at the shelter. He got to drinking beer, and pretty soon he got a little too much and started hitting on Lana, so I had to put him in his place."

"What did you say to him?"

"It's not what I said to him; it's what I did to him. I knocked him on his duff and told him to go home, and said if he keeps sniffing around Lana, he's going to look funny with a .357 hole in his forehead. I'll do it too. Don't you think I won't?"

"What was the outcome of that?"

"He came back down the next day and apologized."

"Do you think he could have murdered that girl somehow?"

"It's possible if circumstances were right."

"What do you know about Long John, Blondie, and Mr. Archie Crabtree?"

"I've had Long John, and his helper Ben, over for a fish fry a time or two. They both love their beer; they must have drunk a case between them. Long John likes cat fish better than bass fingers. His helper is kind of a sneaky fellow that I don't much like. Mr. Crabtree seems to be okay. He helped me once on some legal papers I needed advice on. Blondie I don't know at all. All I know is she is supposed to be great with the blind kids. That's it, I guess."

"Thanks Al. You've been a big help. Let us know if you hear or think of anything else that might help us with this case."

"I sure will, Rick."

We went back up to our motor homes and got in old Knock About to go get us a bite of dinner. The influx of northern folks down here has caused some folks to start calling dinner "lunch." It will always be breakfast, dinner, and supper for me. We went on down to Mama Bell's for a bite, and when we went in and took a seat at our favorite table, Mama herself came over to our table to take our order.

I asked her what was for dinner.

She said, "Southern fried chicken, butter beans, fried okra, collard greens, with biscuits and corn bread."

I just sat there with my mouth open, almost drooling. "Enough," I said. "Bring it on Mama, bring it on."

Jerry said, "Me too."

Mama brought us both a big glass of iced tea with lemon in it. We sat there like two angels in heaven waiting for our heavenly vittles. Soon Mama brought us each a plateful of hot, steaming food fit for kings (southern that is). We both carried on something terrible over that food. My mama used to say the secret to good cooking is just a pinch of sugar. I have found that to be so true in a lot of things I cook. It was really good eating.

Mama loves every minute of our carrying-on over her cooking. She cooks to please people and of course to make some money. She has a couple more ladies she has trained to do it her way now to help her out and free her up to do PR work up front. That's very important to any restaurant. We paid her and tipped her big.

As we were leaving, she hollowed, "Rick, wait a minute." She went in back and came out with something round wrapped in foil. She handed it to me.

"Your pone of corn bread you ask me to cook for you."

I had forgotten all about that, but she hadn't.

I asked, "How much?"

She just shook her head and said, "Take it on home with you and enjoy it."

I said, "Thanks, Mama, and left." I didn't tell her how I would eat most of it. I like to crumble up my corn bread in a bowl of milk and dice up some Vidalia onion over it and eat it like that. Goooood!

Chapter

9

AL'S LAW IS IN FORCE

I was watching this guy who has the camping space down near the pond behind Al's mobile home, fishing for Al's trophy bass. When he or someone else catches a big one and gives it to Al, he puts it in his pond. A lot of guys won't eat the big bass, saying they don't taste as good as the smaller ones, so they give them to Al. (I find that to be true. The best-tasting bass is about two to three pounds or so.) He has some monsters in that pond. They are his pets that he feeds all the time.

About that time Jerry walked up and took a seat under my awning and asked for a beer. I said, "You know where they are, go get us two, you knuckle head, your legs aren't broken." When he came back out of my motor home he handed me one and opened his and sat back down.

"I'm watching that guy down there fishing in old Al's private pond. He's caught several of Al's big bass already. I sure hope Al doesn't catch him at that. It'll be Katy Bar-the-Door."

Jerry said, "You got that right Rick. He will blow a fuse."

"Rick I'm sitting here watching this guy and worrying about catching the killer of blonde woman. Shouldn't we be working on that case instead of watching this guy?"

"Jerry, you know your right and we will, but this is going to be too-good to miss."

Al and Lana were gone to the doctor in Lake Wales, and this guy thought he was going to catch him a big one or two out of there while the coast was clear, not thinking that someone else would tell on him for doing it. He caught a few and took them over to the dock to clean them in the sinks put there for that purpose.

Al and Lana returned sooner than he expected, and, sure enough, the trouble-maker of the camp, that everyone dislikes, called Al and told him. Al walked over there and asked him where he caught his bass.

He said, "Lake Kissimmee."

Al said, "How many did you catch?"

He said five.

Al said, "That will be two hundred fifty dollars. Someone called a minute ago, saying they saw you catch them out of my pond. Pack up right now and leave the camp and don't come back ever."

Al is tough about things like that. One time he had an air boater come roaring into the canal, making a big wake, and stopping at the place on the dock for gas. Al dislikes airboats more than I do.

The guy was drinking heavily, and made the mistake of hollering at Al to "fill 'err up."

Al told him, "No gas sir."

The guy didn't believe him, and said, "I said, fill 'err up."

Al turned and told him to wait right there, then went in the office. Soon, he came back out, walked over to the guy pointed his 357 Magnum pistol at the airboat's motor, and put one round right through the block.

Al went back inside and called the game warden. Soon the game warden arrested the man and took his airboat out of the water and out of the way. Word got around about that and Al had no more airboats dropping by for gas.

10

10

JERRY WANTS TO TALK TO BEN. THE HELPER

*J*erry said, "Let's go to Long John first and ask him more questions about his helper, Ben. Like, say, what is his last name, and where he's from, et cetera?"

Off we went in the old Knock About back to the Blind Camp. I parked in my usual place and went looking for Long John and his helper, Ben. We found them over cleaning the pool.

"Long John, we need to talk to you and Ben some more," I said.

"Okay, I guess," they both said.

"Long John, we are going to talk to Ben a little bit first."

"Sure, go ahead."

"Let's walk over to the bar area so we can sit down."

We walked under the aluminum roof-covered area and sat at a table around the pool. Ben seemed a little nervous for some reason. We had done nothing to make him so.

"Ben, may I ask what your last name is?" I asked.

"It's Martin. Ben J. Martin."

"We want to know where you came from."

"I'm from Georgia . . . Macon, Georgia."

"What did you do up there?"

"I worked on a farm for a while and then worked my way down to Florida. I always wanted to come to Florida. I was up in Haines City and met this lady working there named Janet. I told her I was looking for a job, and she had heard that the Blind Camp was looking for someone, and here I am."

"Did you know the deceased?"

"I've only seen her from a distance but never met her. No, I didn't know her."

"Did Long John know her or socialize with her any?"

"Yea, I saw them talking together several times. I accused him of having it on with her, but he just laughed."

"Ben, I want to tell you right now that whatever you tell us will go no farther than us and will not affect your job in any way."

"Good, I'm glad of that."

"Then what do you think of Mr. Peoples as a person?"

"Not much. He's not my kind of people. He cheats at poker. He lies, and Lord knows what else he is or does. I know he is gone from here in the evenings quite a bit. I heard him talking on the phone to somebody this morning about meeting them at the Dallas Rodeo in Bartow after work. It's a bar and dance club."

"Ben, do you know Mr. Crabtree?" Jerry asked.

"I know him when I see him. By the way, I was out in the pool, taking a swim the night Mrs. Crabtree was found, and saw Mr. Crabtree come driving in from somewhere."

"What time was that?" said Jerry.

"It was right after Long John found Mrs. Crabtree. Somewhere around midnight I think."

"Ben, we thank you. Please call this number on my card if you can think of anything else that might help us solve this mystery and tell Long John we will talk more with him later."

We walked over to the Knock About, and I said to Jerry, "Let's go take a nap, come back this afternoon late, wait on a side road for Peoples to leave this evening, and follow him to where he is going. We might have to be up all night. Who knows? What do you think of that old partner?"

"I think that's a winner, Rick!"

When we got back home, Jerry went into his motor home, and I jogged down to talk to Al a minute. He was standing out on the dock, looking out at the lake at something, when I jogged up.

Hi Rick, Al said, "I'm watching these two guys making noises like a shotgun going off or something that sounds like that. If they don't stop soon, I'm going out there to talk to them. If they are setting off charges to stun fish so they will float up to the top of the water so they can net them, I won't put up with that."

"What did you want with me, Rick?"

"Just wanted to ask what you know about the Dallas Rodeo over in Bartow."

"Just that it's a rough place and a good place to get killed in, I hear."

"This is on the Quiet. I just found out that Peoples is meeting someone over there tonight. Jerry and I are going to follow him and see where it leads."

"You two be very careful if you are going there. Do you hear me good buddy?" Al said.

"I will be taking care of Mrs. Ulrich's boy for sure."

We waited until right before dark and drove over to Lake Tiger Road. We pulled off to the left onto an overgrown, little dirt road. I turned around and pulled off to the side of the road to wait for Mr. Peoples to pass by in his Cadillac, headed for the Dallas Rodeo. We only had to wait about ten minutes, and here he came lickety-split. I waited a moment and then pulled out with my lights off until I got down the road a ways, then I turned them on low beam. He turned right on Highway sixty, and headed west for Bartow.

We stayed back quite a ways because traffic was light. When he got there, he pulled as close to the front door as he could, and we parked off to the left and back a ways so we could see him come out. I have some old clothes in the toolbox across the back of the truck. We got us two old work shirts and two old ball caps and some black makeup to make whisker shadows, to make it look like we needed a shave.

We went in and looked around until we spotted Mr. Peoples at a table over in the left corner with some woman. She was a pretty redheaded woman with stylish clothes and a modern hairdo. She looked well-to-do and not like someone you would expect to see in a place like this.

We were sitting over on the right side with a good view of them. I ordered a couple of Millers for us. We didn't think even our own mothers would recognize us in our getups.

I walked over to the bar and leaned over to the bartender, slipped him a ten, and asked him, "Do you know the lady with the guy over there? I pointed discreetly with one finger.

He said, "She was the wife of a city commissioner at Lakeland, but I don't know her name."

I asked, "Do you know the guy's name?"

He said, "Peter Peoples is a regular."

"Do they meet here often?"

"Yes they do once a week or so."

I went back over to the table and told Jerry what I had found out.

I paid our bill and went back out to the car, and in a few minutes Peter and his squeeze came out. He turned north on Highway 98 toward Lakeland and went about three miles. He turned onto a dirt road and went about a mile to a house. They got out and went in, turned on the lights, and closed the door. They closed the drapes, and we were left with nothing to do. I told Jerry we might as well head back to the camp. He agreed.

Chapter

11

TYING FLIES AND BRINGING BILL UP TO DATE

I sat down at my dinette table with my popper and fly-tying bench. I have a $400 fly-tying vice mounted on it and more material and hooks, et cetera, than I can keep up with.

I love to catch fish on something I've made myself. That's first-class sportsmanship, I think!

This is one bass popper I've been working on and have yet to try it. The body is made of deer hair that floats well. The tail is made of dyed feathers, the legs are rubber, and the eye is plastic with a floating pupil. A piece of monofilament is tied to the eye of the hook and bent around to the shank of the hook and tied, then glued. That makes it weed less so it won't get hung up on the weeds. I fish a lot with this mayfly when they are hatching out in the spring time.

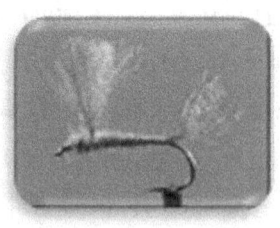

I have to spray silicone or another float spray on it so it will float. The body is not waterproof. What fun that is to catch one of something just about every cast. You never know just what it's going to be. Even shell crackers come to the top for the mayfly, and they hit hard and fight pretty long for a pan fish. Usually you can catch them only with live worms on the bottom of the lake.

For years I fished only with open-faced spinning reels, and then one day I was out fishing when I saw this guy wading and fly-fishing. I stopped to talk with him, and he said he picked up a fly rod about ten years ago and had never wanted to fish with a spinning rod again. I started inquiring about fly rods and fly-fishing, and one day this same guy came over to put in his boat to go fishing. I started asking him about fly-fishing again, and he said, "Come on out with me, and I'll teach you how to fly-fish."

I said, "Okay, let's go."

We went just outside the canal from the camp; he got out of the boat and started getting tackle out for me and him.

He said, "Let's wade and fish. It's easier to fly-fish that way."

I got out of the boat; the water was about waist deep. He handed me a fly rod and got behind me real close. I didn't know what the heck he was doing.

He said, "Hold the rod softly with your right hand and hold the fly line with your left hand and slowly move the rod back and forth, letting the rod do the work. You don't cast a fly rod like you do a spinning or bait-casting rod. You let the rod and line do most of the work. You bring the rod back to about two o'clock and turn loose of your line at about ten o'clock, shooting the line through the ferrules on the rod till it reaches the spot you are casting too."

He took my arm from behind and started moving it like he said, back and forth until I got the rhythm of it, and then he told me to turn loose of the line now, and out it went to the spot I was looking at.

He said, "Now practice that for a while and then start fishing along these reeds and grass. I'll fish on up ahead of you, and if you need me, just call."

Soon I caught a fish and was hooked just like the fish was. I've been fly-fishing ever since.

I spent some time thinking about the dead girl and how she was killed. If she was killed with a large ring, whose ring was it? So I decided to be on the lookout for a large ring on somebody's finger. Boy, what a puzzle this was! I believed that I needed to find out more about her in order to solve this. Old Jerry and I would go back over to the Blind Camp to question some more folks about her and look around a bit. I picked up my walkie-talkie to talk to Jerry. He answered on the first beep.

"Do you want to go with me over to the Blind Camp to talk to some people about Linda Crabtree?" I asked.

"Sure do, Rick, and I are ready to go right now."

"Good. Come on over."

We left right away, and when we pulled into our parking place, there was something happening with a lot of folks running around every which away. We got out and ran over to the pool area and asked this guy we had never seen before, what had happened.

He said, "This little blonde girl named Becky Lake drowned in the pool."

Oh, my Lord! What a nice little girl *she was*, I thought and blind too, how could this be? "Who was in the pool with her at the time?" I asked.

"I don't know for sure."

Jerry saw Ben over at the other side of the pool and pointed him out to me. We walked over to where he was and said hi to him.

"Ben, were you present when Becky Lake drowned?" I asked.

"Yes, I was cleaning out the filter for the pool when I heard someone holler."

"Who all was present at that moment around the pool?"

"Let's see, I remember two or three more people were there—this new guy named Ted something and his wife and son. Oh yes, there was about three or four of the blind kids in the pool then with the swim instructor trying to teach them how to swim. Mr. Crabtree was here, and Long John was here helping me."

"Did she die accidently or what?"

"I don't know if she could swim or not. Her instructor would know though."

"What's her instructor's name?"

"Her name is Goldie Manning. I think she is new here like me."

"When did she come to work? Did she come before you or after you?"

"She came before me."

We went over to talk to Goldie. She was a very cute girl of about twenty-one, with beautiful, long blonde hair and a golden tan, in a bikini. She had brilliant-white teeth. She was refreshing to look at.

Jerry said, "Wow, she looks better than most movie stars."

We told her who we were and showed her our credentials.

I ask her how Becky could have drowned with her being present.

She said, "I was down at the shallow end, and Becky was at the other end in the deep water. This is an Olympic-size pool, you know. When the little kids and I got out of the pool for some refreshments, I looked down into the pool and saw something, dove in, and swam down to it, and saw it was Becky. I pulled her out and gave her mouth to mouth, but it did no good. I couldn't revive her; she was already dead."

"Goldie, could she swim?"

"No, she couldn't swim at all. She was only holding on to the sides, testing the deep end and trying to get her courage up, I guess. I had my hands full with the three or four other blind kids who can't swim to notice her struggling to swim. I thought she was just fine when I last looked at her."

"Were there any other people in the pool at the same time you, the others, and Becky were in?"

"Yes, some of the time some of the new people, several regulars were in and out as well as Mr. Crabtree, who went in and out several times."

"Okay, Goldie thanks for talking to us. You've been very helpful. Here is one of my cards, call me if anything comes up we should know about."

As we were headed for Archie's motor home, Ben caught our eye and motioned us over to him again. We walked back over to him and he said, "You know, fellows, I just remembered Long John getting himself all sweaty and dusty helping me, so he took a swim to cool off after helping me."

"Was this while Becky was in the pool?"

"Yes, it was, but he didn't stay in long."

We said bye to Ben and went on over to Archie's motor home to talk to him some more.

Jerry said, "You know, Rick, Becky was a pretty young lady. How old do you think she was—about fourteen?"

"That's a pretty good guess I would think, maybe fourteen or fifteen."

I knocked on Archie's door. No one came, so I knocked again, and then Archie opened the door and said hi.

"What can I do for you, boys?" he said.

"We want to ask you more about your wife and her habits," I said. "What did she do around here to pass the time?"

"She read a lot, drank a lot, and sunbathed quite a bit. She used to take a folding recliner behind the motor home on the bank of the pond to sunbathe and read. We used to go over to that restaurant on Lake Rosalie quite often to eat. They have pretty good food."

"You mean you didn't eat down at Mama Bell's restaurant?" I asked.

"Yeah, some, but Linda didn't much like her food."

"Where was Linda from?"

"She was from New York City."

"Oh well, I guess that's the reason she didn't like Mama Bell's.

Did you know Becky well?" I said.

"No, I didn't know her too well." Archie Said.

"She told us you were very friendly to her and that she went to your home often and even babysat Albert once in a while."

"Yes, she did some, but my wife Linda took care of that."

"They said you were over at the pool when Becky drowned."

"Yes, I was for a while. That was a shame what happen to her."

"Did you go in swimming while you were there?"

"Yes, I did for a little while, but not while Becky was in."

"Goldie says different. She says you were in and out of the pool several times at the same time Becky was in."

He shrugged. "Well, maybe I was and didn't notice."

"Okay, Archie, that's all we need for right now," I said. "Oh, by the way, did you see Long John go in the pool during this time?"

"Now that you mention it, I did, but he wasn't in for long."

We left and went back to our camp.

"Jerry, do you think some of the help that works there over-heard Becky talking to us that day in the dining room and told Ben, Long John, Archie, or Mr. Peoples and others, what we said?"

"I don't know, but I've been thinking how easy it would be to swim underwater, grab Becky's foot, and drag her down deep in the pool until she drowns, then swim down to the shallow end and get out. It's such a big pool nobody would notice it, it could be done real easy, nothing to it."

The next morning Jerry was still down in a blue funk, so I went to see Bill Dade to let him know our progress. I told him about all I had found out about Peter Peoples; Long John; Ben Martin, the helper; Linda Crabtree and Archie Crabtree; Albert, the boy; Becky Lake, Old Jack Cutlet, the coroner; Clyde Lewis; Camp Fins; Archie's maid and neighbors; and the Dallas Rodeo.

He said, "Boy, you have been busy, haven't you?"

"I'm just trying to get back to fishing, Bill, that's all. Miss it."

"I found out that the Crabtree's were contemplating getting a divorce, but I think it was being held up because she was trying to take half of all he owned."

"That's interesting news, Bill. You know, I've been talking to Jerry that maybe this might be a semi-serial killer case. You know the killer doesn't leave stuff behind, doesn't take stuff from the scene, but he kills nothing but blondes, that's what driving me crazy."

"Let me call in one of my specialists on the subject of serial killers."

He punched a button on his phone and said, "Trace, come to my office for a minute, please."

Soon the door opened, and this guy who had that seasoned detective looks like he just might have solved many cases, walked in.

Bill said, "Trace, you know Rick, right?"

Trace nodded and said he had met me briefly a few years ago, but I didn't remember him.

"Well, Rick is working the Blind Camp case for us," Bill said. "He's wondering why a serial killer that has a thing for blondes, never takes or leaves anything behind. You know like a signature thing left at each scene, or takes something away from the scene. Maybe, like the blonde's clothes or jewelry or something like that."

Trace said, "Well, there can be many reasons why he would do such a thing, and most of them will have something to do with his childhood. Maybe his mother was a blonde, and he loved her deeply, but she was cruel to him. Maybe beat him and locked him in a closet for days or something, but he loved her so much he forgave her over and over. Who knows with some of these weirdoes?

You know Rick, "It's a little early to be thinking serial killer, isn't it? The FBI tagged serial killers, a term they made up in the seventies for those who had committed three murders over an extended period of time with cooling-off periods in between, during which their other activities seemed to be ordinary."

"Thanks much, Trace. You can go now." Sheriff Dade said.

"It was nice seeing you again, Rick, and good luck on your case."

"Thanks very much for your help, Trace. I think it will help me some."

"Rick, keep at it until something breaks, okay?"

"Okay, Bill, I will. Take it easy, old buddy."

When I got home, I got out a couple of New York strip steaks and started up my gas grill. I called Jerry and asked him if he had any baking potatoes, and he said he did.

"Would you wash up a couple for us and fix us a salad?"

I asked him to rub the potatoes with olive oil, sprinkle them with seasoned salt, and wrap them in foil for me to cook on the grill. He said he would and hung up. I got the grill cleaned, hot, and ready for the steaks. I had turned down the heat to cook them a little slower than I usually do so everything would be ready at the same time. I sprinkled some good seasoning on the steaks and placed them at one end of the grill, because I was going to cook the potatoes at the other end of the grill at a different temperature.

Soon Jerry brought over the potatoes and salad and a couple of ice-cold Miller High Life's.

I said, "That's my boy, that's my boy."

We leaned back in our chairs and cooled it. I checked the steaks and potatoes and turned them over. We had another Miller, and soon the food was ready to eat.

I took it into my motor home and set it on the table. I had laid out two place settings earlier. We proceeded to enjoy us a fine meal fit for a king. When we finished, Jerry went over to his motor home, and I cleaned up, washed up, and went to bed.

Chapter

12

RAIN AND MORE RAIN

The next morning when I woke up, it was raining like it was pouring out of a boot. I looked out, and it looked like the bad weather is set in for the day. I turned on the TV to get the weather, and the weather man said a rain-squall had blown in from the Atlantic, and that it would rain all day and night.

Rick thought there is nothing much I can do about working the case as long as we have this kind of weather.

I called Jerry and woke him up, which he didn't appreciate, and told him what the weatherman had said. I told him, "It's a good day to read or sleep."

Jerry said, "I'll sleep, if you don't mind."

I said, "I'll read my favorite author, John D. MacDonald."

I made myself a couple pieces of cheese toast in the toaster oven and a cup of instant coffee, and then went back to bed to read. I was reading the Deep Blue Good-By. John D. had lived down on Siesta Key below Sarasota, Florida, before he died. A good many authors live down there. They have a group meeting place at a restaurant on the island to get together and discuss their latest endeavors. It's a good way to air your ideas and listen to others efforts.

I read quite a while and then drifted off to sleep. I woke about three o'clock and walked down to the docks with a big golf umbrella to see what was going on. There was a group sitting down there, drinking beer and telling lies. They were drinking Bud, and I just don't like it, so I didn't take one. They were talking about the Army Corp of Engineers digging all the canals between all the lakes. With the locks they are putting in, they can hold back the water until hurricane season comes and then let it out so water won't flood everything. The only thing that's wrong with that is that when the grove owners and sugarcane people want water they can open the locks and have at it. That messes up the fish bedding in shallow water the way they like to do. The engineers have really hurt fishing in more ways than one.

Rick said, "Boys, I can remember wading in the old natural river that was still the way God made it and fishing was fantastic. I have pictures to prove it. "

"Once two of my buddies—Garland, Willard—and I had just waded down the three miles of the river from Lake Tahopikaliga to Lake Cypress, and I was beat, so I sat down in my boat for a rest and anchored it. We each had a stringer almost full of bass and blue gill.

"We used six-foot stringers then, until one day I was wading in Fryers Cove at the south end of Lake Tahopikaliga. I had two or three fish on my six-foot stringer, and I felt a pull on it, so I reached back and pulled it back and kept on fishing, then something pulled it again and pulled me over in the water. I reached down, trying to untie the stringer and couldn't, so I just slid my belt off and gave him the fish, stringer, belt and all. It was a big gator that did it. It about scared me to death. That is when I started using twelve foot stringers." They all laughed at that, "Saying, tell us some more stories Rick."

Rick said, "I think we had something like one hundred fish between us. I had a rope from my boat tied around my waist and my stringer tied to the boat. There was no size or number limit then on how many fish you could catch.

Willard and Garland kept on fishing around the west side of Lake Cypress and still catching fish. I sat there in my boat, eating a sandwich and drinking a cold Miller. There was two telephone poles sticking out of the water about eight feet, and they were about three feet apart. An old commercial fisherman had built a shack there years ago, and the poles were the only thing left.

I picked up my spinning rod with a purple worm on it and cast it right between them. I let it sink and gave it a little twitch, *Bam*—a big bass hit it and started back towards the posts with it. I jumped out into the water with him, trying to keep him from getting around the two telephone posts. Then he turned and headed for the foot of the outboard motor. I was able to turn him. Finally I wore him out before he did me. Pulled him in and reached for him with my thumb and stuck it into his mouth and clamped down on his lower jaw to paralyze him. I stood there, admiring him, and then took him off the hook and weighed him. He weighed eight pounds eight ounces.

I put him on the stringer and got back in the boat to finish my sandwich and beer. While I'm eating, I sat there wondering if that is a bed down between the posts, and if it is, can I cast over it to the other side and slowly crank the worm through the bed. That makes them mad as fire. I picked up my rod and did the exact same thing I was thinking and—Bam—another one hits it. I jumped back out of the boat and repeated what I did before and got her in, and she weighed eight pounds. Nobody believes this story, but it really happened but has never happened again in all the years I've been fishing, and that's the truth if I ever told it. I have the picture to prove it."

They all said, "That's a good one, Rick. Got anymore?"

"Yea, but I'm saving them for another time."

It was still raining cats and dogs. I ran back up to the motor home and dried off.

I called old Jack, the coroner, to find out if he had done an autopsy on Becky Lake yet. Jack answered the phone.

He said, "Just now finished. She drowned."

"I know that, Jack, but how did she drown?"

"That's your job to find that out."

"Mine is to just slice and dice them."

"You mean you didn't find any evidence of foul play?"

"No, I found no foul play at all Rick. I'm sorry. I did the best job possible, but no dice."

I can't believe she just drowned right there in front of God and everybody.

I fixed myself a sandwich with liver cheese, a sliced Vidalia onion, sliced tomato, lettuce, and some Dukes Mayo on toasted honey-wheat bread. That makes a good sandwich. Watched a little TV and then took a soothing nap with the rain hitting the flat roof of the motor home.

I've loved the sound of rain hitting the roof ever since I was a real little boy and we visited my Grandma Grace's home down in Pendleton, South Carolina. She had a two-story home with a tin roof. I used one of the upstairs bedrooms so I could hear the rain better at night. One night two of my uncles, Edward and Alton, were sleeping in one bed, and a cousin, Maxie, and I were sharing the other bed in that same room. I woke up late one night and saw Edward sitting in one of the big windows with his legs hanging out over the side, looking like he was going to jump. So I hollered at Alton to wake up and get him. Alton ran over to the window and grabbed him. When he woke up it scared him also. It scared him and us. He had been walking in his sleep.

Chapter

13

BILL DADE HAS SOMETHING NEW

The rain had stopped the next morning when I woke up. The whole park was flooded with rainwater. I couldn't get to the restrooms and showers, so I had to shower in my little one in the motorhome bathroom, and my elbows almost punched holes in the walls of the shower. I'm a big guy at six three and 250 pounds. This shower was made by and for a midget.

I made some coffee, cooked me some bacon, scrambled eggs, diced me up some extra-sharp cheddar cheese, and made grits and honey-wheat toast. That is fine eating, I'm telling you.

Bill Dade called and asked me to come in to see him. I said, "Okay, I'll be there this morning." I called Jerry and told him what I had found out about Becky from Old Jack not finding any foul play at all, and he couldn't believe it either. I asked him if he wanted to go with me to see Bill Dade, and he said yes. He said he would be over in a minute. We had to take our shoes and socks off and wade to old Knock About.

If we were going fishing now, we would have looked for places where the water was running into the lake. I remember one time I went fishing after a hurricane. I lived in Orlando, in East Orlando Homes, at the time, so Garland and I went down past the east side of west Lake Tahopikalika to Saint Cloud, then south on some country roads to Coon Hammock, and then down a pig trail to the east side of Lake Kissimmee on the bank of North Cove. Parked on a high spot and waded out to the edge of a drainage ditch running into the lake. I mean the water was just pouring out of the fields and ditches into the lake everywhere you looked.

Garland and I waded around the mouth of this ditch and caught one bass after another. We had never had so much fun ever. We were hollering and laughing and just catching the heck out of the bass. I've never seen the like of it since.

I hollowed at Garland, "How many have you caught so far?" "I've just caught my twenty first bass. Man this is something isn't it!"

I've caught them fast and furious a few times since but nothing like that day. We caught so many; we were throwing them back below a certain size. They were feeding on worms and small snakes that were washing into the lake from the fields, so we were using plastic worms. Back then we made our own worms. We bought bottles of liquid plastic and heated it in an old pan until it was real runny, and then we poured it into molds we could buy and made our own. Some worked well, some didn't. It was fun catching fish using something we made ourselves.

We got to Lake Wales Sheriff's Department and went right on into Bill's office.

He said, "Hi, fellows. I couldn't believe that about Becky. I can't see how she could drown without attracting attention to herself. Any way things are looking up. We found out that Long John had been arrested for rape back in his hometown of Robertsdale, Alabama. He was working for this farmer who had a farm out off of College Avenue that worked a lot of Mexicans. The farmer gave him a little hut to live in while he worked there. This pretty, young Mexican girl kept hanging around there and slipping out at night to come see him. She would slip into his hut and spend the night with him. This went on for a while until her mama caught her at it, and the girl hollered rape. He got out of it on a technicality.

"Also, we found out Archie has been married before. Soon, his wife went missing and has never been found."

I said, "Boy, this puts a new light on things, doesn't it?"

"It sure does, Rick."

"Let's see. It makes both of them look guilty, doesn't it? I think I'll call my good friend, Barry, up in Greenville, South Carolina, to do a little snooping for me about Archie, to see just what he can find out about him for us. You don't suppose we have a serial killer on our hands, do you, Bill?"

"Could be, Rick, could be. Ask your friend to find out if his first wife was also a blonde."

"I sure will, Bill."

"Yes, I think he does, but I'll ask him. Okay, Bill, see you later."

Jerry and I drove on through Lake Wales and toward home, stopping at Mama Bell's for some dinner. She had fried fingerling catfish on the menu, along with French fries, hush puppies I gave her my recipe for them, and she uses it, and some good coleslaw chopped instead of shredded, my recipe also. Her catfish are the kind that commercial fishermen catch for some restaurants. They are split-tail cats they are called channel cats that feed up in the water like a bass, not on the bottom like the other catfish. They are a game fish and are fabulous to eat.

This reminds me of a story about these channel cats. I lived in Brandon on a two-block-long dead-end street. I heard from one of my friends about this commercial fish house that bought and sold channel cats and had plenty of fingerlings for sale at a good price. So I went over to the town of Kissimmee to the commercial fish house and bought about thirty pounds of them for a fish fry I planned to invite the whole street to it.

When I got home, I moved things around in my freezer in the garage and in the house, and made room for them. I had a ping-pong table and about three or four card tables. I borrowed several more. I made up invitation cards and had my son, Tony, deliver them to each and every house on the street, and I called some of these folds myself.

The evening of the fish fry came, and I was busy making up hush-puppy mix— heating the oil for frying the fish, salting and peppering and breading them. Jill set out the slaw, baked beans, plates, napkins, forks, spoons, and drinks of all kinds, plus Miller High Life.

I started cooking fish about thirty minutes before arrival time. It smelled good around the Campbell home, and I couldn't wait until my friends and neighbors had tried the channel catfish fingerlings for the first time. People started showing up, and soon we had a crowd. Everybody had something to drink, and we soon started eating. Things were going great until this woman from up north, who had just moved into the neighborhood, said, "Mr. Campbell, these fish have bones in them!" It got real quiet then.

All I could think of to say was, "Thank God they do, because they wouldn't be fish if they didn't."

That was the end of the good time, because I looked around and thought, Most of my neighbors are from up north. That particular woman had eaten only frozen fish out of supermarkets all her life. That's when I realized how lucky I was to have experienced outdoor life in Florida. Needless to say, we ate fish for a week at my home after that fiasco.

When we got home, I called Barry and left a message for him to call me, that it was important, and that I needed some help. He evidently screens all his calls, because he called me right back after about five minutes.

"Hi, Rick, how's things? You'll never guess who I played golf with this week."

"You're Cousin Tony and I did eighteen holes."

"I played with Arnold Palmer."

"You're kidding me, right?"

"He was at our golf classic, and I got to play with him. What a golfer he still is."

"Rick, I had the privilege of helping get up over five million dollars for charity this year."

"Barry, that's wonderful, you doing that for charity."

"What did you call for, Rick?"

"First, let me ask you if your PI license is still in effect."

"Yes, it is, Rick."

"Good. Do you by chance remember the lawyer by the name of Archie Crabtree, whose wife went missing a few years ago and was never found?"

"Yes, I do. I remember it well."

"The reason I'm calling you is to see if you can find out just what happened to her if you can. You know so many people there in Greenville, South Carolina. You can come up with something for me. It's important to me because I'm working on the case where his new wife died or was murdered down here.

"Rick, am I hearing you right, that he married again and his new wife was murdered?"

"She sure was right here where they have their blind boy in a camp for the blind."

He's been living down in Brandon for a few years and has a practice there.

His wife was found on an island in a pond near where I live on Lake Tiger. Her left leg and arm were hanging in the water, and a gator ate part of both. I know the sheriff of Polk County and he hired me to find out who or what did happen to her. The coroner says she died of natural causes, but I don't believe that at all."

"Wow, I wish I was down there so I could work on it with you. It sounds like an interesting case."

"I have my sidekick, Jerry, who is helping me out, but you can help me more up there by finding out what you can about the disappearance of his first wife.

"Barry, find out if she was a blonde. Let me know when you have something for me, okay?"

"I sure will, Rick. I have to do most of the cooking since Maxie had her heart attack. Everybody sure does love your chili-dogs."

"I can think of one or two I can send you when I get time. How is Maxie doing, by the way? Fine, I hope."

"She's getting better and better, Rick."

"I'll call you later."

"See you."

Chapter

14

BARRY GOES TO WORK

*B*oy, this is going to be some challenge to find out what Rick needs to know. It was nice to hear from Rick after such a long time. It's great that he has enough faith in me to do a little sleuthing for him up here in Greenville. I'm sure glad I got my Private Investigator license renewed awhile back.

Let's see, who do I know that would know Archie Crabtree? Oh, I know who would remember him and possibly will be of some help to me, my lawyer friend, Henry Philpan.

I called his office and told his secretary who I was, and she put me right through to him.

I said, "Henry, this is Barry. How have you been keeping?"

"Oh, fine, Barry. How 'bout yourself, how are you doing?"

"Listen, I want to buy you a steak at Charlie's Steak House tonight after work."

"I never turn down one of Charlie's steaks. What time?"

"About what time do you finish up?"

"Say, would about five o'clock be all right?"

"Sure will. I'll see you there."

It was two thirty, so I had time to fix Maxie something before I left. I showered and dressed, and by that time it was 4:15; I had just enough time to drive into Greenville to meet Henry. Henry and I go back a few years. I had him do some work for me a few years back when I sold my brokerage businesses, and he did good work.

I got there right at five o'clock, parked, and went in. He was already there and had us a good table in the quietest part of the restaurant. I shook his hand and sat down. The waiter came right over, and I ordered us a good wine. He got right to the point.

"What can I do for you, Barry?"

"Henry, I need some help."

Just then the waiter came back with our wine and took our order. We both ordered porterhouse steaks, baked potatoes, and salads.

Henry was always trying to get me to go into this investing club with him and a few others that met once a week, buying and selling stocks, etc.

He had a lot of fun in one a good many years ago with his Dad, Erwin Philpan, Morris Newton, Ron Ulrick, and about six others. He said Ron Ulrick was the secretary and book-keeper. "I believe he had a son down in Lake Wales, Florida, named Rick Ulrick," he said.

"Well, I'll be. That's who I'm helping out and the reason I asked you for help. Rick Ulrick called me last night and asked me to help him find out all I could on Archie Crabtree and his missing wife from up here. It seems Archie remarried, and now his new wife is dead. Found lying out on a little island, naked and chewed up by a gator. The coroner could find no evidence of murder and is calling it natural death, which Rick doesn't believe. This happened next door to where Rick lives at Al's Ramp and Camp, on Lake Tiger about a mile north."

"Okay, Barry, I owe you one for helping me out on that case a few months ago. I liked old Ron Ulrick and would love to help his son out. I'll have my investigator look into this and see what he can come up with for you. He is very good at his job. He will dig up all the dirt on Mr. Crabtree. You know Digger McGee over at McGee's Funeral Home might be able to help you some. I played a little poker with him a couple times, along with Archie and a couple others."

"Thanks, Henry. Give me a call when you have something, and I will call Rick."

Our food came, and it was good as always at Charlie's Steak House. I went on back home, walked in the house, and saluted old Robert E. Lee hanging on my wall. I went to check on Maxie. She was watching TV, so I went in to check my e-mail and had ten from Rick alone. When did he get time to send all of these e-mails? I worked on my latest book for a while and then went in with Maxie to watch a movie and went to bed after that.

The next morning I got up and fixed Maxie and me something for breakfast.

I remembered Rick telling me about this dish he came up with for breakfast I liked. I opened a can of corned beef hash, got out two small Corning ware bowls, put the corned beef hash into them, and packed it down using a spoon. I made an indentation in the hash of the size that would hold an egg broken into the little hollowed out place. First, I placed the bowls with hash in the toaster oven, turned it to broil, and cooked the hash until it was brown and crisp. I slid the bowls out and broke an egg into each. I salted and peppered the eggs, and put the bowls back in the oven until the eggs were just done with the yolk still a little runny. I called Maxie for breakfast and fixed some toast for us. I like to dip my toast into the yolk of the egg as I eat the hash and egg. That makes a good breakfast.

Then I got dressed and went to see my cousin Bicie to see if he could remember something about Archie that might help. When I got to his house, Bicie was busy with another one of his projects. I told him about

Rick Ulrick calling for help and explained things to him.

Bicie said, "Barry, you know Digger McGee of McGee Funeral Home. I knew Digger as well as anybody could. Archie and Digger hung around together all the time. They used to have a poker game every week in the funeral home building. I ask him one time why the funeral home and he said it's always quiet and nobody bothers us there. I bet he can help you out some."

"Yeah, that's what Henry Philpan told me. Thanks, Bicie. I'll go talk to him."

I went over to McGee's Funeral Home, and sure enough, Digger was there. I went into his office, and he said, "Well, I'll be, Barry!"

"Need some help for a friend of mine, Rick Ulrick?"

"I know Rick, but I didn't know he was in town."

"He isn't. He called me last night from his place on Lake Tiger in Florida and asked me to help him find out all I could on Archie Crabtree. It seems Archie got married again, and now his new wife has been murdered."

"That sorry son of a gun left here owing me over ten thousand dollars he lost to me playing poker. I'll help you anyway I can, Barry. I gave him a key to the funeral home so he could get in when he and some of his friends wanted to play poker. You know, Barry, he was hateful to his wife all the time. She could never do anything right in his eyes."

"You don't suppose he would kill his wife, do you?"

"Who knows? If he got enough booze in him and got mad enough, I guess he could."

Chapter

15

LONG JOHN

*J*erry wanted to go talk to Long John about the rape charge up in Alabama. We got ready to go to the Blind Camp when the phone rang, and it was Barry. He told me all he had accomplished up there in such a short time.

"Boy, Barry, you get right after something, don't you? You say Archie played poker at the McGee Funeral Home and was given a key to it so he could go there when Digger was out of town? Yes, and he left town owing Digger ten thousand dollars from playing poker and never paid him back?"

"Henry Philpan helped me out quite a bit and steered me to Digger. He liked your dad and wanted to help you. He wants me to join him in this investing club he and some of his friends have started. He said he enjoyed the one he and his dad and your dad had a good many years ago."

"Yeah, Dad liked the Philpans very much and made a good bit of money with them. Thank you very much, Barry, for the help, and call me if you get anything else, okay?"

"I will, Rick, and you're welcome. By the way, before you go, I found out that his first wife was blonde."

"Oh good, because we think we have a semi-serial killer on our hands."

"What do you mean semi-serial killer, Rick?"

"Well, for one thing he's not leaving something behind or taking something away with him like most of them do, or killing the same way every time that causes them to be called serial killers."

Jerry and I went on up to the Blind Camp and went looking for Long John. He was down at the pond with a long-handle rake, pulling hyacinths out of the water around the edge of the pond. We walked over and asked if we could talk to him.

He said, "Sure can. Let's go over to that table in the shade under that big oak tree."

"Long John, we heard you had a rape charge against you up in Alabama, and we want to talk to you about it. What happened, and how did you get out of the charge?"

Long John's face and bald head turned red when rick asked him about the rape charge. He started swinging his knees back and forth, back and forth like he was really nervous.

"Well, Mr. Ulrick, I was working for this farmer up in Robertsville, Alabama, and he was good to me. He gave me this little, old hut to live in rent free if I would fix it up some, and he would pay for the supplies to do it and me too. I was sort of a boss of the Mexicans in the fields as well."

Long John had his finger interlocked and was twisting his thumbs, first one way round and then the other.

Long John continued, "Soon this little, old Mexican girl kept coming around, paying attention to me and me to her. She was a pretty thing, and I liked her. After a while she started coming to see me at night after everyone was asleep and crawled into bed with me. I didn't kick her out, because she seemed to want it worse than I did. Then one night her mother missed her and the next night followed her. She jumped all over that girl, and the girl said I raped her. I had this friend that lived in the hut next to mine tell the law he had never seen that girl come to my hut, so the girl didn't have a leg to stand on since her mother had no witnesses. So I got off. That's when I quit and came down here."

"That's quite a story, Long John."

"Mr. Peoples said you had good references."

"Yes, the farmer I worked for gave me a nice reference."

"He didn't frown on your trouble with the girl?"

"No, because I think he was romancing her too. You see, we thought her mother was trying to get her married off to an American so her daughter could stay here in America and possibly herself too."

"Thanks, Long John, for the information. Oh, by the way, do you swim?"

"Yes, I do. Why?"

"Did you ever swim in the pool?"

"Sometimes I did when everyone had gone in after dark."

"Thanks. See you later."

Oh, Long John, can we come into the pond from the lake in my bass boat?"

"You sure can, Rick. The lake belongs to the state and the pond too."

"Okay."

"Jerry, let's you and I go back to base and take a ride in my bass boat. We will cut off the outboard motor and tilt it up so it won't drag in the shallow water going into the pond from the lake. Then I'll put the trolling motor out at the edge of the reeds. We will troll on in with it while the foot of the outboard is raised up."

We went down to Al's Ramp and Camp, drove on out to where my boat was, got out of the Knock About, and left the keys in it in case Al needed to move it for some reason. Got in my bass boat, let it down into the water with the hoist. I Started it up, backed out into the channel, and pulled up to the gas hose on the dock to refill the tank with gas and oil. We told Al where we were going and about how long we would be gone. I did this about every time I went out in the boat so he would know where I'm supposed to be in case I don't come back in a reasonable length of time.

I drove over to the Blind Camp, cut my motor, and had Jerry put over the trolling motor so we could work our way back into the pond. I flipped the tilt switch to raise the foot of the outboard motor so it wouldn't drag on the bottom as we trolled through the shallow channel into the Blind Camp pond. The way was pretty clear of weeds and stuff, so we made it in just fine. As soon as I got inside the pond, I turned on my depth finder and was surprised at how deep it was. It was anywhere from six to twenty feet deep. The deepest part of Lake Tiger is only about ten feet.

I got out one of my fly rods with a wild-cat popper on it, and fished around the north side of the pond, and caught a couple of nice bass and several blue gills. Jerry had his rod out after I caught the first bass and caught a couple of nice bass. We needed to remember this place when the wind got up sometimes out on the lake. It would be calm in here.

We trolled around the little island where the naked blonde, Linda was found, to see if we could find any evidence from out in the water since we had already walked around on it looking. We didn't find anything from the boat either. We shortly went on back to camp and put up the boat, got out our fish, and went up to the sinks to clean them for dinner.

Al said, "That's the fastest fishing trip I've ever heard of, and look at the fish you caught. What did you do—have a fish basket out there somewhere?"

"Aw, Al, we just fish fast," I said.

"Bull, nobody is that fast."

We drove back to the motor homes, and I got out the big cast-iron skillet for frying fish, and hush puppies. I had some slaw in the fridge. I made up some of my batter for the fish. I made up some cornmeal and onions, with other ingredients, and made hush puppy mix.

Jerry got the electric burner hot outside for the big frying pan and filled it about half full of canola oil (no cholesterol). I brought out the batter and hush-puppy mix so he could start cooking the fish and hush puppies.

I called down at Al's and invited him and Lana for dinner.

He said he would take us up on that. "Be up there in a minute or two," he said. The two were added for Lana's sake, since he knew it takes women longer to get ready to go anywhere. They came up after a while, and I got them a couple of ice-cold, sweat-running-down-the-sides-of-the-bottle Miller High Life's.

They both said, "Thanks."

I asked Lana how she had been doing.

She said she had been keeping busy helping around the camp, teaching the old ladies how to get back up to speed to go back to college. When their partners pass away, they need something to do. "I have my bridge games one night a week and the ladies' missionary society meeting one night," she said. "I'm forever cooking some kind of new dish I just have to try. I love to cook."

Soon the food was ready, and we had some kind of good meal. I asked Al how they were doing with the camp.

He said, "You know, Rick, we don't have to run this place. We just like people, and this place makes us a bunch of money. We have some business properties we lease out. We are buying up all the land we can around the lake. We already own several thousand acres, and Josh, our foreman, takes care of a thousand head of cattle for us on our land. The green belt law, you know, saves on taxes."

Jerry said. "Boy, I didn't know you guys owned all that."

"I hope you can keep up with it all, Al." I said.

"It won't be long before Lana and I are going to do what you and Jerry do. That's as little as possible, right?"

"Al, we work hard at our PI work."

"Uh-huh. I know, I know."

Chapter

16

IT'S BACK TO THE GRINDSTONE FOR US

Ick said, "We are back to square one with this case. We need to solve it quickly if we can.

"How are you doing on the Blind Camp case?" Lana said.

"Oh, some days we make a lot of progress and some days hardly any at all." I said.

"Yeah, Rick, it does go from feast to famine." Jerry said.

"Jerry, I wonder where Becky Lake lived," I said. "I'd like to know something about her parents and more about Becky."

"Let's go back up to the camp and talk to Mr. Peoples about Becky," Jerry said. "What do you say?"

"Okay, buddy, suits me," I said.

Al and Lana soon got up to go, and we said good night. Jerry went to his motor home, and I went into mine after we cleaned up our mess. I washed up and went straight to bed.

I heard someone knocking on my door the next morning and hollered, "Come in." It was Jerry with two cups of coffee and a smile on his face.

"Uh-huh, I got you back this morning, didn't I? How did you sleep Rick?"

"Not to good, Jerry. I've been tossing and turning all night, thinking about this case we're on."

"Well, did you come up with any ideas?"

"I glad you asked that because I want to run something by you to see just what you think of this theory of mine. Do you think we have a serial killer on our hands? Oh, I don't mean the usual kind of serial killer who leaves a sign to let you know it was him. I'm thinking more like one that uses women a short while and then tires of them and then kill them for some unknown reason. Some of the women he just kills, but he marries some, keeps them a while, and then kills them for some unknown reason. Does that make any sense at all to you, Jerry?"

"Yeah, I guess so. You think our man is such a person?"

"I don't know, but I'd like to do some research on it and see if Bill Dade has ever heard of such a thing. Give me a few minutes, and I'll be right with you, okay?"

"I'll wait on you in the Knock About."

When I finished dressing, I had me a piece of cheese toast made with extra-sharp cheddar, toasted in my toaster oven. Then I finished my coffee and went out. Jerry was behind the wheel of the Knock About, ready to go.

I said, "You feel like chauffeuring this morning, Jerry?"

He said, "I didn't think you would be awake enough to drive this morning, so I think I'll drive."

"Thinking of me and my sleepless night, huh?"

"You, I was thinking about Mrs. Churchill's boy this morning. Are we still going to talk to Mr. Peoples?"

"Yes we are, and maybe some others too."

We got there just as breakfast was about over and found Peoples in the dining room, eating alone. We walked up to him and asked if he would talk to us a while.

He said, "Let's get some coffee. I didn't have enough myself."

We walked over to the big coffeemakers and drained out three cups for us and Jerry. Then we got a cinnamon bun and walked over to a quiet corner so no one could hear us.

I started right off with a question for Peter Peoples. I didn't want him thinking too long about why we were back and talking to him again. If he was guilty, we wanted him to feel a little pressure. That sometimes makes people do crazy things.

"Do you remember the names of Becky Lake's parents?"

Peoples said, "The father's name is Donavon, and her mother's name is Reba. They live somewhere in Riverview. I have Becky's file in my office."

I asked if we could look at that file, and he said "Sure."

He said, "You know, guys, we really miss Becky around here. She was so helpful with the little kids. They just loved her. What a tragic thing, her death."

We went back in his office while he looked for the file. "Here we go," he said, handing it to me.

We took the file and read where Donovan and Reba lived. It was in Riverview on Shady Lane. The phone number was in there so I wrote it down and gave the file back to Mr. Peoples. We thanked him and left.

We got in the Knock About I called the number. Mr. Lake answered and I gave our condolences for his daughter's death. I asked if I could ask him a question or two, and he said yes. I asked if he knew if Becky had had any love interest in Archie Crabtree.

He said, "None that I can remember. He was too old for her."

"I know that, but I just wondered if he ever came on to her before."

"She did complain about the way he was talking to her one time when he brought her home from babysitting his son, Albert."

"What was he saying to her?"

"She said he told her he could love her more if she would let him have sex with her. I got mad as fire and was going to talk to his head about that, but she said, No, I can handle him. Don't you worry?"

"I told her I didn't want her to baby sit for them anymore, and if he laid one hand on her, I'd sic the police on him."

"Don't worry, Daddy, she said, he won't hurt me. I can handle him. She did say she wouldn't sit for them anymore."

I thanked him and hung up. I told Jerry what he'd said, and he had a fit. "Well, that sorry, low-down bastard! He should have his butt kicked clear out of town by yours truly." interjected Jerry.

About that time, there came a bolt of lightning like a cannon shot right near where we were. Jerry was so keyed up he jumped like he had been shot. I looked around at the sky, and it was black. Black birds sat in a row way down the telephone line the way they do when bad weather is coming.

"Let's go back to our motor homes and turn on the weather to see what we are facing," I said.

I turned off Lake Tiger Road onto Paul's Road and went about a mile down the dirt road into Al's Ramp and Camp. We went into my motor home real quick, because the wind was blowing terrible. I turned on the TV and got the Weather Channel. The weatherman said we had a hurricane named Connie coming up from the islands at a fast clip. It was already a category-three hurricane, and it was headed diagonally across the state right toward us.

"Oh, boy, what do we do now?" Jerry asked. "What do we need to do first?"

"We need to roll up our awnings and put everything away around the homes. We both have nylon straps and screw-in anchors that will help some."

"Come on, Rick, let's get busy quick," Jerry said.

"Okay, Jerry, help me get my awning in, and I'll help you with yours. These big oaks around here will protect us from the wind some, but let's hurry and screw in our anchors, pull down our nylon straps good and tight. Oh yes, we need to check the bass boat to see if anything needs to be done there, like put the canvas boat cover inside the boat up under the dash console. Tie all the rods and reels to the boat."

Jerry asked me if I had any gallon jugs we could put water in, in case the power went out.

"I have a few."

He said he did too. "We will fill them with water and store them in the motor homes."

"We each have enough groceries to do us," I said.

"I think I will clean out my little bathtub real good and fill it with water. That will give us enough to bathe with for a while."

"That's a good idea, Rick."

The weatherman just said it was coming ashore at Port Saint Lucie, northwest, straight toward us.

"We will just have to pray it turns one way or another and misses us," I said to Jerry.

Already the Spanish moss was blowing toward the northwest, and the lake had swells in it. I moved the Knock About in a position where the tail end would face the oncoming storm. If it got too bad, we would try to make it to the concrete-block washhouse or restrooms. They would withstand more than a motor home.

Jerry and I watched the weather and news on my TV. I fixed each of us a can of soup. We drank Miller High Life from the refrigerator.

Our motor homes were turned broadside to the storm, and there was nothing we could do about it. That was just the way the camp was laid out, so everyone could see the lake and docks. We could already feel the wind rock the motor home a little bit. The weatherman said a front was coming in out of the Gulf from the west. That was good because we thought it might push Hurricane Connie more to the north so it would miss us.

I looked out my dinette window and saw some Styrofoam minnow bucket go flying by, so the wind had picked up quite a bit. I was praying the storm would turn to the north or go back out into the Atlantic. It was raining cats and dogs, and the wind was blowing the rain almost horizontally. The rain was beating against the big window beside my dinette. Debris was blowing all around; plastic, Spanish moss, and paper were flying through the air.

About that time the weatherman said the leading edge was about over Yee haw Junction, which is about forty miles from us. It was getting closer to us. No matter which way it went, we were going to feel the effects of it quite strongly.

"Jerry, if you want to, you can pull out that couch," I said. "It makes a bed or use the overhead bunk, so you can bunk in with me tonight. I'll sleep in my bed in the back bedroom."

I took another look out at the lake, and it had huge swells of rolling waves. I saw a piece of galvanized tin roofing go flying off the boat dock's roof. Then good news came over the TV. The front coming east out of the Gulf did its work and moved the hurricane more to the north. Then it turned it more toward the northeast and the Atlantic just like I had prayed.

I just said, "Thank You, Lord."

Boy, did we get rain and wind all night long. It really rocked the motor home for all it was worth. If I hadn't had it strapped down, it would have gone over on its side, I have no doubt. The next morning we had moss, twigs, and leaves all over the place. Some limbs and trees had been blown down.

We had work to do this day. The roofs of our motor homes were covered with all kinds of stuff. I attacked that first, because I have a ladder on the back of the motor home for that purpose. We got everything cleaned up around the motor homes and put the awnings back out and the chairs too. We went down to the docks to see what damage the storm had done to them and found Al there gathering up sheets of roofing that had blown off. We helped him gather it. Our boats were all right and dry. Connie was a tough old girl.

Chapter

17

BARRY IS HELPING
ME AGAIN

I called Barry up in Greenville, and asked him to go over and talk to Digger and ask him if they ever kept metal stuff they found in the crematory. I had an idea that the first Mrs. Crabtree might have had some metal on her—partial plates, screws, or jewelry. They keep a record of stuff they find.

He said, "Okay, Rick. I'll go over there today and see for you and call you back."

"Barry, what got me started on this crazy idea is, the other night I was thinking about the labor leader Hoffa that disappeared and was never found. I always did think that somebody knew an undertaker that let them cremate him. I've heard that story more than once. It made me think of Mrs. Crabtree never being found and Archie having a key to McGee's Funeral Home. He could have used it to cremate the Mrs. one dark night."

Barry called me back in two hours and said, "Rick, on the day Mrs. Crabtree went missing, Digger found that the crematory had been used and not cleaned out of all the ashes. That was very unusual, so he kept the ashes in a jar with a date on it just in case there was a mix-up somehow. I looked through the ashes, and what did I find but a ring with a rose carved in it. It would have melted, but it was made of titanium. Now all you have to do is find out if she wore a ring like that."

"Wow, thanks, Barry. That's good news. I'll let you know what I find out. Send me that ring ASAP."

"I will, Rick; I'll send it one-day airmail."

"Thanks, Barry. I owe you one."

The ring came the next day just like it was supposed to. Now I had to see if the first Mrs. Crabtree had worn such a ring. I guessed I needed to fly up to Greenville and work on this myself. I went over and told Jerry about my good fortune.

He said, "Gee, Rick, that's great. What luck, huh?"

"Jerry, I think I'll fly up to Greenville to see about finding who made this ring for who."

"That's going to be expensive, Rick."

"You remember, Sheriff Bill Dade said expenses paid. I'll call Barry to let him know I'm coming and what for. Maybe he will pick me up. You can keep snooping around down here to see what you can come up with if you would, Jerry."

"Sure thing Rick, I'll take you to Orlando tomorrow to catch your plane."

"I'll make reservations for in the morning about ten a.m." I did, and they had one out at 10:10 a.m.

I made it and was set to go. Then I happened to think of this guy in downtown Main Street Lake Wales. He ran a small jewelry shop there and was a wiz at working with metal.

"Jerry, do you remember that jeweler on Main Street Lake Wales named Gus? Let's drive in to Lake Wales and pay him a visit."

"I'd like to go Rick. Let me change clothes in case I run into a sweetie."

"Yeah, I know."

I went into my home, washed up, shaved, and got dressed fairly well considering what Jerry will dress like. I combed my hair and put on my dress shoes. I went out, cranked up old Knock About, and waited on Jerry. Soon he came around the corner of my home wearing a Hawaiian shirt, white pants, white shoes and a Panama hat. Boy, what a sharp dresser he is. He just might get hooked up with a sweetie dressed like that.

I whistled at him, and he just grinned from ear to ear. We drove on into Lake Wales right on by Mama Bell's without stopping. I pulled into a parking space right in front of Sparkle Jewelry Store.

Lake Wales beautified Main Street a while back with a brick circle planter with tall palms in it. To slow down traffic, they put it right in the middle of the street, where you had to drive around both sides of it. They put in planters all along Main on both sides of the street with nice trees and flowers in them and park benches too. It looked really peaceful.

We went in to see Gus about the ring. We were the only customers, so I said, "Hi, Gus."

He looked up from what he was doing and grinned. "Hello, Rick and Jerry, What bank, have you two robbed now? Ha."

I put the ring in his hand and asked him, "How can I find out who made this ring and where it was made?"

He looked at it with his loupe and said, "Huh, made of titanium and engraved with a very special tool with a rose on the top of it?"

He looked up at me and asked, "Where are you thinking this was made?"

I said, "Greenville, South Carolina, I think."

He said, "Well, maybe one store might do this. It takes a very special and expensive machine to do this work. Look for a guy like me that works with metal a lot. I'm not talking about selling, buying, and sizing rings, etc.; I'm talking about creative jewelry, making it yourself. That's the guy you need to find."

"Thanks, Gus, you've been a big help to us," I said and slipped him a twenty. I glanced at Jerry. "Expenses paid, Jerry. Expenses paid."

I went back out to Highway 60, turned left to Highway 27, turned left, and went one mile to this place called Snow Birds Salad Bar. They have a great salad bar. We ate and headed back home. Jerry wanted me to go on up to the Dallas Rodeo to see if that redhead was back in there, the one who was with Peter Peoples the other day. I do believe Mr. Jerry wants to get himself fixed up with that redheaded woman. So I went in with him, and sure enough, there she was in almost the same seat she was in the other day.

The bartender saw us and brought us two Millers. I've always wondered how they do that. How do they remember what everybody drinks? It amazes me. In a minute out walks this number one honey that went over and sat down with Red.

We walked over, and I said, "We were sitting over there, talking about you two, and I thought it would be nicer to come over here and talk to you face-to-face."

The redhead said, "Suit yourself, but we have already been spoken for."

So we went on out to the old Knock About and pointed it toward home. I drove along Highway 60 east a while, then remembered that Wal-Mart had been getting in some Tiger Cat poppers. So I stopped, and we went in to see if they had any, but I didn't find any. They sell them for something like $1.87. Somebody must have some people chained up and must be feeding them bread and water while they make these poppers. I wouldn't think about making one for less than $8 or $10.

Jerry was awful quiet and sulking. I ask him, "What is the matter with you?"

He said, "It's a crying shame to get all duded up like this just to go to Wal-Mart."

I laughed so hard at that, my sides started hurting. His pride was hurting him. He had been shot down . . . and him looking his best. Oh boy!

18

18

IN MY HOMETOWN WITH MY LONGTIME BUDDY, BARRY

*B*arry picked me up at Greenville-Spartanburg International Airport in his Hummer. Man, what a vehicle that is. Rides good, and that is a surprise to me. Barry says he likes it better than any vehicle he has ever owned.

He got me a room at the Hyatt downtown. I've stayed there several times before and liked it very much. It was a good place to hunt for that one jeweler I was looking for. I checked in for four days, and Barry and I went to my room. I went in the bathroom to water my lily, wash up some, and then visit with Barry.

I went back down to the lobby to visit with Larry awhile and have something to drink. I saw Barry over at a large sitting area and stopped at the bar to order us a couple of cold Miller High Life's and nacho chips and salsa brought over to the table I pointed at. I walked over and shook Barry's hand and sat down across from him.

"Thank you very much, Barry, for picking me up and making my reservation for me. That was mighty kind of you to do that. How is Maxie doing? How far from here do you and her live from here?"

"We live about fifty miles from this hotel. We live just on the other side of the lake. How was your flight coming up?"

"Oh fine, just fine. What did you think of my idea of finding the jeweler that made this ring?" I asked, pulling it out of my pocket."

"I think it's a great idea, Rick, and I might know just the man you are looking for."

The bartender brought over what I had ordered and sat it down on the table between us. I signed the ticket with my room number on it and handed Barry a beer and he took a nacho and scooped up some salsa and popped it in his mouth.

"Good, Barry. Listen to this theory I've been mulling over to see what you think about it. Have you ever heard of a serial killer who kills women and doesn't leave a sign that it was him? But he kills women for some unknown reason?"

"Maybe he's killing someone, say, like his mother over and over again, thus a serial killer first class. I'm beginning to think that's what we have here."

"Let's check on the jeweler in the morning. I'm tired after a late night and the plane ride up here. Meet you right here at eight for breakfast. Is that okay with you?"

"Sure will, Rick. See you then."

I called Pizza Hut and ordered their thin-crust pepperoni pizza. I got a Coke out of the fridge to go with the pizza, ate and then went to bed.

The next morning Barry called the room and said, "They have a nice buffet down here if you haven't had breakfast."

I told him I would be down in about ten minutes. I put on some sport clothes and went down-stairs. Barry was drinking coffee and reading the Greenville News. He asked, "Sleep well?"

"Sure did. Like a rock. Have you eaten yet?"

"Yeah, I had a bagel and cream cheese. They have country ham this morning if you like that."

"Do they? Wow, yes I do, and some scrambled eggs, grits, and whole wheat toast will do me fine."

I told the waitress that same thing, plus coffee right off the menu. I forgot the buffet. I don't like the scrambled eggs at a buffet. The cooks add milk and whip them up just like they are making an omelet. That is not scrambled eggs.

She brought the coffee right away.

"Where do we start first, Barry?" I asked.

"I know a guy on south Main Street that has a shop that makes all kinds of jewelry for people. Uncle Mack used to buy aunt's jewelry from him a lot. He is very good at his craft, and he might help us."

I finished breakfast, and we piled into Barry's Hummer and headed down Main Street. What a change they had made to it.

They have planted Trees and planters with flowers. It sure looks nice now. "Barry, do you remember when Main Street used to be four lanes? Boy, what memories this street brings back. Hayward Mayan's was the place to buy your clothes. For your shoes you had Patton, Tillman, and Bruce; and Thom McCann. Western Auto. Remember the orange juice place where they squished the oranges for fresh juice? Oh, and the Carolina Theater. The café on the left— don't remember its name—and the S&S, Meyers-Arnold, Belk Lindsey, Poinsett Hotel, and Woodside Building, to name a few."

Barry laughed and said, "Nothing like coming home again is there, Rick?"

"You can say that again."

Soon we were over the south main street bridge. "Barry, remember who used to be in that building there?"

He said, "Who?"

I said, "Henry Elrod, the photographer. He did my high school annual and many of my family's photos."

"Yeah, he did many for my Uncle Mack and his family."

"You went to Greenville High, didn't you, Barry?"

"Yes, I did, Rick."

"The most famous person I know that went there besides you was Paul Newman's wife, Joanne Woodward."

Barry said, "Boy, what a memory you have, Rick."

"Didn't you use to get hungry when you went down Augusta Road, smelling first the Krispy Kreme Donut Bakery and then Classen's Bakery? Oh boy, what smells they gave off?"

Barry just laughed and said, "You got that right, Rick."

Barry parked in front of this old building, just south of the bridge. The old, faded sign said, "Creative Jewelry." We got out and went into the past of maybe forty years ago. In the back was an old man hunched over a desk light with a vise, hammer, and other tools. He was working away at something.

Barry said, "Vinnie Swartz, you got a minute?"

Vinnie looked up and squinted at Barry for a minute, then said, "Who's asking?"

"I am, you old penny-pincher you."

He looked up again. "Barry, come here and sit your boney butt down and tell me how you've been."

"Vinnie, we need a little help if you can. By the way, this is my friend, Rick Ulrick."

"I'm glad to know you, Rick."

"I'm glad to know you, Vinnie." I reached into my pocket, pulled out the ring, and told him it was found in a crematory; I asked if he knew who made it.

He took it and stuck his loupe in his eye. He looked at the ring for a minute and said, "I made this some years back for some lawyer's wife. I think it was Crabtree."

I said, "Are you sure?"

"Sure I'm sure. I would know this ring anywhere. It's one of a kind."

"Why in the world would a man have a titanium ring made for his wife? Titanium is ugly to me."

"Well, Rick, you see, it was covered in twenty-four-karat gold. The heat from the crematory melted it all off and left the titanium."

"Oh, okay. Now I understand. I turned to look at Barry and said, "We got him, Barry. We got him!"

"Thanks very much, Vinnie, for your help. Can I use you as a witness if I need to?" Rick asked.

"You're very welcome. Come back when you can. Yes, I will help you catch a killer of women."

"Barry," I said, "let's go on back up to the hotel. Looks like I can get out of here in one day."

Barry drove us back to the hotel where we parked and Barry said, "I thought you might stay around for a few days. "Rick.

"I would if I wasn't working on this case. Great job you did, Barry. Thank you very much for all your help. What are you planning on doing the rest of the day?"

"I have to go do some office work and see about Maxie. Would you like to come home with me?"

"I would, but I need to go see my brother, Jimmy, and visit another friend of mine while I'm here. I plan on leaving tonight, and I'll catch the hotel bus to the airport. Barry, please thank Henry Philpan, our lawyer friend, for his help for me."

I gave old Barry a hug and said good-bye, then headed for my room. I used the bathroom and called Jimmy. He answered on the second ring.

"Whattttt Cheu Doinnny?" I said.

He said, "Whattttt Cheu Doinnny?" and laughed. We have been greeting each other like that for years.

I said, "I'm at the Hyatt. Come and get me."

He said, "I'll be right there."

He showed up in about thirty minutes. I got in his van, and we headed for Berea and the old home place. Sandra and Mylinda were there, and I got to see all my nephews and nieces. I hugged them all and played with the boys a while, and then Jimmy and I went over to see my nephew, Chris. He was at home, working on a cover for a new book on his computer using the new cs6 program to do it. I hugged him, and we visited awhile.

It was getting on toward supper time, and I told them I wanted to go to the Apollo and get some of their chili dogs. They laughed, and away we went. We went inside and ordered up. Their chili dogs are somewhat like ours at Campbell's Dairyland in Brandon, Florida.

I told Jimmy I had to get back to my hotel and pack because I was leaving this afternoon. They said they thought I was going to stay for a few days. No, I was working on a case, I said, and needed to get back. Jimmy took me back, and we said our good-byes, and he left. I called Jerry to meet me at the Orlando airport, then packed, checked out, and caught the shuttle for the Greenville airport.

Chapter

19

DISAPPOINTMENT

I arrived in Orlando after a very smooth flight. Jerry was all excited and wanted to know all about the way things had been going. I filled him in on what had happened, telling him about the jeweler saying he had made the ring and me telling Barry we had Crabtree now.

"What do you mean, Rick, that you've got him? Did you find evidence that he did do it?"

"Sure did. The jeweler told me he made the ring for Crabtree."

"But, Rick, that doesn't prove he did it. Anybody could have killed her and broken into the funeral home and cremated her. You know, pick the lock. We need real proof that it was him that did her in."

"Jerry, how in the world are we going to find proof he did it?"

"Don't ask me."

"Let's stop by Mama Bell's for some chow on the way home."

"Okay, that suits me."

We pulled into Mama Bell's, and she was busy.

"Looks like word is getting around about her good food," I said.

We got out and went in. The place was packed except our usual table, and I couldn't believe that. Mama saw us and came over.

She said, "I've been expecting you two any minute."

"How could you know we were headed this way?" I said.

"Oh, female intuition, I guess. I saved your table."

"I see you did and thanks. What do you have on the stove, Mama?"

"Well, to start with I have some of the best fried chicken you have ever sunk your teeth in. The chickens are small two-to two-and-a-half- pound fryers that I cut up and marinated overnight in buttermilk. We took them out of the fridge today, salt and peppered them, rolled them in self-rising flour, and fried them in a great, big, old cast-iron skillet. They are crispy, tender, and delicious as they can be.

"Next, I have a beautiful macaroni pie made the way you like it with cheese, milk, and eggs. It will knock your socks off. Some big, old butter beans cooked with a ham hock for flavor and corn on the cob. Plus I have one of my yummy cherry pies for dessert."

"Bring it on, Mama," I said. "Bring it on."

The next morning we were having coffee out under my awning, listening to the birds singing and watching two pairs of Florida cranes. They slowly walked around, all regal looking with those long necks and long legs, digging with their beaks for mole crickets. The mole cricket is a strange-looking insect. It is light brown in color, with its front half looking like a cricket and its back part looking like a grub. It is much larger than a regular cricket, and it always burrows underground a little ways to eat the grass roots.

The camp has some Bahia grass, and the mole crickets dearly love it. The cranes find where they have been burrowing under the ground, eating the Bahia grass roots, and they use their beaks to dig for them. They must be tasty because the cranes spend hours eating them every day, and that is good for the grass.

I could hear the airboats in the distance. Not far enough away to suit me. I hate the things. They constantly run over cover I use for bass fishing, bending it down and breaking off the reeds and stuff like that. They are making a mess of things. They are a nuisance.

"Jerry, did you get anything done while I was gone?"

"I went up to the Camp for the Blind for a while, just hanging around, seeing what I could see. Talked to some kids, and that's about it. I keep wondering about Long John feeding us so many tips. Seems kind of fishy to me; telling us about several suspicious things. Do you think he is the guilty one?"

"I just don't know, Jerry."

"Since what we call two murders happened there, even though we have *three* blondes' dead, it is the best place to try to find an answer for them. I have to call Bill Dade and report what progress we have made. Then we will go back to the Blind Camp to see if we can dig up something."

I called old Bill and told him what went on in Greenville, and he agreed with Jerry that we would need more than just the ring.

"Let's walk down to the dock and check in with Al," I told Jerry.

Al was busy cleaning out his minnow tank.

He said, "Hi, Jerry. Hi, Rick. What are you two doing out and about?"

"We just came to pay you a visit and find out what's new around here," I said.

"Rick, do you remember those two guys making all that noise out in the lake that day?" Al asked. "Well, I heard them again up on the north shore doing the same thing. I got in my boat and ran up there real quick, and they were doing what I thought. They had gun powder, foil, and waterproof squibs to make bombs. Attached a big sinker to them, lit them, and tossed them in. Any fish anywhere near were stunned and floated to the top, and then they netted them.

"I had my .357 with me. I told them I was the game warden and was arresting them and said, 'Come with me.' I followed them into camp, making a citizen arrest. I ordered them to sit in their boat for a minute and then went in the office to call the game warden; they came in about five minutes. They must have been headed this way anyway. He arrested them, took their boat and car, and left."

"Wow, wish I had been here," I said. "I would have helped you. You can't catch fish that way. You say they were up at the north end, huh?

"Yeah, they were just two lowlives. Jerry, let's you and I get on over to the Camp for the Blind."

Chapter

20

MARY CONTRAIRE

We got in the Knock About, tooled over to the camp and our usual parking spot, got out, and sashayed over to the pool area. Goldie Manning, the swim instructor, was there with several blind children; she was teaching them not to fear water. We sat and watched her for a while and saw she was well liked by the kids. She is one good-looking woman.

I asked Goldie if we could talk with her a while after she was finished with the kids.

She said, "Sure, I'm almost finished with this class now. Be right with you after I change into something dry. I'll stop by the restaurant and get us something to drink. What would you like to have?"

I said tea and Jerry said Coke.

In a few minutes Goldie was back with our drinks. She had slipped into a swimsuit that was less revealing but still skimpy. She is a doll, all right; pretty as a speckled pup. I asked her where she was from.

"I'm from Cocoa Beach, Florida. I started here last year about this time. I worked as a lifeguard on the beach for several summers while I was in school and then for a while after school. I'm twenty-seven years old and still single. I have never met Mr. Right yet. Most guys are afraid to make a commitment to marriage. I've had some handsome guys want everything but that, and I won't give it to them. I love helping these blind kids get over their fear of the water and learn how to swim. It's rewarding for me to do so."

"Tell us about the day Becky drowned. What were you doing right before and after she was found?" Rick asked.

"I took four kids with me about one hour after lunch to the pool to get them used to being in water and got them to hold onto the side and do some kicking and stuff like that. I'm working toward teaching them how to swim. We did that for a while and then did some floating and dog-paddling."

Goldie pushed her hair back behind her ears as she was talking to us. She was beautiful even with her hair wet.

Goldie continued, "They are progressing nicely. Then we got out, dried off, and had some refreshments. I noticed something on the bottom of the pool, so I dove in to check it out. To my horror, it was Becky Lake lying on the bottom. I pulled her out and tried to resuscitate her but to no avail. She had turned blue and looked terrible. I called someone to go tell Mr. Peoples."

Jerry asked, "Were the kids and you the only ones around the pool that day?"

"No, there were others. Mr. Long John, Mr. Ben, Mr. Crabtree, and several new people I hadn't met yet were there."

"Did you see any of them go in the water during that time?"

"Yes, several of them did. The new family did, the husband and wife and two kids. Mr. Crabtree and one of the other blind boys did after he had finished eating."

Jerry said, "Did any of them get near Becky?"

"The blind boy and Mr. Crabtree did."

"Do you know the boy's name, Goldie?" I asked.

"It's Charlie Smith."

I wrote that down and asked which of the people who went in the pool spent the most time around Becky.

"Mr. Crabtree did and one of the new men spent a good bit of time around her."

"Did you see him do anything he shouldn't have with her?" Jerry asked.

"No, I didn't."

"If you can think of anything else, please call me at the number on this card, and thank you for your cooperation. You have been very cooperative; it has been a pleasure interviewing you." Rick said.

"You're very welcome and now I must get back with my little future gold medalist."

"Jerry, let's go over to see if Archie is still here and ask him a few questions. What do you say?"

"Yeah, like ask him what his first wife was wearing the day she went missing and if she wore any jewelry that day."

"Hey, Jerry, that's pretty smart of you. You're a pretty smart, man at times, you know that?"

We went over and knocked on Archie's motor home door, waited, and then knocked again.

"Just a minute," somebody said.

Soon a woman neither of us had ever seen before came to the door. She had long, beautiful blonde hair and wore the flimsiest negligee I have ever seen.

She said, "Oh, I thought you were somebody else." She closed the door while saying, "I'm going to get a robe on."

We looked at each other and raised an eyebrow each. I whispered, "*Another blonde all ready*," and stood there until she got back, opened the door again, and asked what we wanted.

"We are looking for Mr. Crabtree. Is he here?" Jerry said.

"No, he's gone to Brandon for a couple days to catch up on some of his business doings."

"Are you related to him?" I asked.

"May I ask who you are?" She said.

"Sorry, I'm Rick Ulrick, and this is Jerry Churchill. We are private eyes working for the sheriff's department on Mrs. Crabtree's case." I showed her our credentials.

"I'm here keeping an eye on Alfred, Archie's son. I'm a friend of Archie's, Mary Contraire."

"I see," I said. "May I ask where you live and your address and phone number?"

"I've lived in Brandon all my life. I live on Overland Drive and my phone number is on it."

"Are you married?" Jerry asked.

"No, I've never been married."

"Who were you expecting a while ago?" I asked.

"I was expecting Archie to come back from Brandon."

"Did you get along with Mrs. Crabtree?"

"No, I didn't. Why?"

"I was just wondering. We need to know. Do you know who might have killed Mrs. Crabtree?"

"No, I don't. Wish I did."

"Here's my card. Call me if you come up with anything that you think might help us. Thanks." We left.

I said to Jerry, "Man, that Archie changes women faster than I do underwear."

"Rick, I hope you don't wear underwear that long!"

"I don't wear any underwear at all, but I do bathe. I love the freedom. In Florida the least clothes you wear, the better off you are."

21

MAYBE THINGS ARE COMING TO A HEAD

We left the Blind Camp and drove down to Mama Bell's for a late breakfast. Our usual table was waiting on us, so we went to it and sat down. Mama had a new table tent of Plexiglas sitting on it that said,

Table Reserved for Rick Ulrich and Jerry Churchill.

We looked at each other and laughed.

"Can you believe it, Rick?" Jerry said.

"No, I can't, for sure. Mama has gone overboard now."

Mama saw us and came over with a big smile on her face and said, "Now I don't have to worry about saving you two a table."

She gave us two menus and asked what we wanted to drink.

I said coffee and Jerry did too. Mama brought two steaming cups of good, fresh coffee. I took a look at the menu but asked Mama if she had some corned beef hash, and she said yes.

I said, "Mama, can you get your cooks to griddle some for me until it's crisp on both sides? Tell them to soft-scramble me some eggs and don't use the ones that have milk in them that they have beaten up for omelets.

You know,(country scrambled). Also some cheese grits and honey-wheat toast."

"Make that two, but I want some Texas toast instead." Jerry said. Okay boys, I'll be right back with your coffee."

"Jerry, I've been thinking that we need to talk to Albert some about his parents just to see where that leads. What do you say?"

"I had almost forgotten about him. Sure. We need to talk quite a bit to that young lad."

I looked around at the inside of Mama's restaurant, trying to figure out what was different about it. She had painted the walls a soft off-white and put up some pretty curtains in the windows, small flowers on each table, and a large vase of flowers on the checkout counter. She had a friend of hers paint some airbrush pictures of Florida outdoors on the side walls; they looked fabulous. She had changed the ceiling tiles for some new, modern ones that looked great. She had added some of her best food on a take-out menu, which will at times help Jerry and me when we are in a hurry. She had put a fairly large-sized sign on the back wall with a pretty good saying on it and a nice picture of herself too.

Mama Bell's Restaurant has been doing business since 1995.

We want you to come back to see us

real soon and are looking forward to serving you again.

"Now that's a nice touch, isn't it, Jerry?" I said, pointing it out to him. He shook his head yes but said nothing. I had to look at him to see what in the world had his attention so. I followed his line of sight to see what he was looking at, and it was that good-looking redheaded woman Peter Peoples had been with at the Dallas Bull that night.

I said, "I wonder if she is meeting Peter here today instead of the Dallas Rodeo"

Jerry said, "I bet she is, and if she is, this is another opportunity for us to tail them."

It wasn't long till Peter popped out of his car, came in, and sat down with her, giving her a kiss on the cheek. I was sitting where I could keep an eye on them while I ate. She must have worn the hottest pants in town. We ate slowly so we could finish about the same time they did. Soon they finished their meals, left a tip, and headed for the checkout to pay the bill. We hung back a little while they paid and left.

We said bye to Mama Bell, paid, and left too. We followed them back toward Lake Wales to the Sleep Easy Motel. After they went to their room, I went in the office to check the register and see what names they had used. They had signed in as Mr. and Mrs. Cecil Sly. I gave the desk clerk a ten and asked him how long they were staying.

He said, "They usually only stay for a few hours and then leave, but this time he paid for two days."

Now I wondered what was going on with these two and how I was going to find out. Her husband could have found out about her and left her, so she was staying down here so she could talk it out with Peter and decide what to do next. I thought that just might be the case.

"Jerry, is that downtown spy shop still open?"

"It just barely is, Rick."

"Let's go see if he still has one of those listening devices he had the other week. I think we need one now."

We went down off Highway 60 into downtown to the Spy Shop on a side street, went in, and asked to see one of those listening devices. Our luck was holding, as he had one left. We bought it and asked for a demo on how to use it. He showed us until we understood it, and then went back to the motel. I drove around back so I was behind their room, got out the listening device, and pointed it at one of their windows. I put on the headphones and heard Peter talking right away.

Chapter

22

IT'S GETTING
JUICY NOW

Peter was saying, "Oh, how I've been missing you, Millie."

"Umm, I've been missing you too. I love it when you do that. Don't... Don't ever stop."

Jerry had been looking at me, grinning and shaking his head.

He reached for the headphones and said, "Let me listen to some of that, Rick."

"Okay, you can listen for just a second or two."

He put them on and immediately started laughing and slapping his knee, saying, "Hi ho, Silver, away."

I reached over and grabbed the headphones back. I didn't want to miss something important while he was listening to them.

I put the phones back on and heard Millie say, "Oh Peter that was so good. I want to be with you forever."

I heard them stirring around and then heard him say, "Maybe we can, Millie. Maybe we can. But we have to get this thing settled with your husband first so we can get married. I need to be with you all the time, not just once a week or so."

She squealed, and he laughed and said, "Just think, we have two whole days to just be together and love each other. I have Long John looking after things at the camp and the others to back him up, so we can let our hair down and enjoy each other. Your husband should have his divorce papers by tomorrow, and you have your appointment with your lawyer three days from now. Soon we can get married and go on our honeymoon."

"Oh, I can't wait. Where are we going on our honeymoon, Peter?"

"Don't worry about it. I guarantee you are going to love it, sweetheart. I have it all planned out for seven wonderful days at a fantastic place."

"Come here you," she said. Then there came another squeal, then just the sounds of lovemaking, which I wasn't interested in unless it was me making the sounds.

I said to Jerry, "Let's go. This all just sounds like two lovebirds enjoying each other. Nothing fishy here."

We went on back to the Blind Camp to question Albert about his parents and see what he thought and knew about the murder of his mom. We saw him in the mess hall, playing some game with another boy. I walked up to them, told them who we were, and asked Albert if he would talk to us a little while alone. He said, "Sure," so the other boy quietly left us.

I said, "Albert, do you know about your mom and what happened to her?"

He said, "Yes I do, and I still cry for her at night when it's quiet and I'm alone."

"Do you know who might have done such a thing to her?"

"Only one person ever got mad enough to do that to her, and that was my dad, but I don't think he would go that far." Albert said.

"Well, if you can think of anything that will help us, please call us at the number on this card. See you later, Albert." "Okay, glad to help."

We went back into town to the new gun store called Cypress Bay Head Sports Shop, east of town near Wal-Mart, to look at their gun offerings.

"I want to trade in my thirty-eight for one of those smaller nine millimeters," I said. "I'm going to keep my hideout what I wear in my ankle holster. What do you carry now, Jerry?"

"I still have my police special thirty-eight snub nose."

"I wouldn't mind having one of those nine millimeter babies myself. I hear they have a new Glock C that helps you keep aim during rapid fire."

We stopped right in front of the front door, got out, and went in. Who was waiting on customers but Lana, Al's wife from the fish camp? I poked Jerry in the ribs and said, "Look who's running this place. Lana."

"Well, boys, are you surprised to see me here? I just bought the place; going to put my son, Chuck, in it to run it for me. We are going to put in a firing range out back."

"Lana, I believe you will make it go. I know one thing though; Al had better treat you nice now, you having all these guns."

She laughed and said, "What can I do for you two?"

"We are interested in the new Glock C for both of us," I said.

Lana said, "Let me get the person I bought the store from. She is staying with me for two weeks until I get used to everything about running the business. By that time Chuck will be here from California to run it."

She went in the back and returned with this absolutely beautiful blonde with skin-tight jeans, a cowboy shirt, a cowboy hat, and boots. I loved to watch her walk, and she was just about my age. I began to have some old feelings again.

She smiled at me, and I felt like I needed a place to sit down. Wow, what a woman. Jerry was just standing there, looking real intelligent with his mouth hanging open and almost drooling. If she had asked me right then what I wanted, I couldn't have told her for the life of me. She had that much effect on me.

Lana said, "This is Pammie Carlyle, who sold the store to me, boys. Pammie, this is Rick Ulrick and Jerry Churchill. They want to look at the Glock C model nine millimeters, okay? I told them you knew all about them."

"Let's go over to the glass showcase and get you a couple to look at," Pammie said. She reached in a drawer behind the counter, pulled out two boxes, and laid them down on a plastic handing pad in front of us. I opened my box, and there was the most beautiful pistol you will ever see. I picked it up and was amazed at how small and light it was.

Pammie said, "It holds seventeen rounds and will shoot at a rapid rate. The Glock C model has two slots cut in the top end of the barrel for some of the escaping gases to go upward to help hold the barrel down during a high rate of fire, to give you a tighter pattern. Also, it's so small you can wear it in a shoulder holster, and it won't show. The list on it is five hundred ten dollars. Do you have anything to trade?"

"Yes, we both have these thirty-eights we want to trade in on these Glocks."

She took them, unloaded them, and looked them over real good. She said she would take our guns and $800 plus tax for the two Glocks, unless Lana wanted to give us anymore off.

She turned to Lana, and Lana smiled and said, "Give them another ten percent off for old time's sake."

I said, "Thanks, Lana. Does that suit you, Jerry?"

"Yeah, sure does, and thanks, Lana."

Lana said, "Let's fill out the paperwork, and when it is recorded, I'll bring them home to you after I close that day."

I said, "Fine." Pammie gave me my receipts for the guns. I thanked her, and then we said good-bye; I winked at Pammie, and we left.

It was getting on toward supper time, so I asked Jerry if he was hungry and would like to stop at Mama Bell's for some of her fine vittles. Jerry said, "My stomach is thinking I forgot about it."

We headed out Highway 60 toward Mama Bell's and then home. We got to Mama's, pulled into the same space we had last time, went in, stepped over to our table, which was ready for us, and sat down. Soon Mama saw us and came over with that beautiful smile of hers to see what she could do for us.

"Well, boys, how was your day? And what are you going to have this evening?"

"You know, Mama, I've been craving one of your vegetable plates," I said, "with some of your corn bread and a big glass of your iced tea. What kind of veggies do you have today?"

"Boy, are you in luck, Rick. I just happen to have some fresh cantaloupe, corn on the cob, fried okra, some pinto beans cooked with a ham hock in it, turnip greens, and cooked cabbage and Vidalia onions. How does that sound to you?"

"I'll take the loupe, fried okra, pinto beans, and cabbage and onions with some corn bread, please," I said.

Mama said, "Would you like some of my chow-chow pickles to go with those beans, Rick?"

"You mean, you made some more of that good chow-chow Mama?"

She shook her head yes.

"I said bring it on Mama, bring it on."

"I didn't, but my new cook did, and it's my recipe. I hired her from over in Plant

City after a friend, Freddy Johnstone, told me about her. I had to pay her a bunch to get her, but she can make anything I can and sometimes better. I'm proud to get her. I tell her a recipe one time and she's got it. Remember that old motel that closed down last year on the south side of Highway 60? I bought her one of those little, old efficiencies dirt cheap for her to live in and a pretty good car to get back and forth. I still hold the title for both until I know her better. Mama can't be taken for a fool. She seems to be grateful for all I've done for her, and I am for what she has done for me. She frees me up to do more of what I'm doing right now with you, talking to my customers."

"Now just wait a minute. What about me for a change? I need to order too you know." Jerry said.

"I'm sorry, Jerry. I should have let you go first," I said.

Mama said, "What are you going to have, Jerry?"

"I've been craving one of your big turkey Cubans all the way—hot pressed—some fries and a big glass of Coke."

"Okay, I'll go put in your order and bring your drinks."

She was right back with our drinks, and we had our food not long after that. I asked her to sell me a jar of that chow-chow to take home. We ate our fill; I told Mama it was the best yet. She just smiled, and we said good-bye and went back to our homes.

As I was fixing to go in my motor home, Lana pulled up, having just gotten home from the Cypress Bayhead Sports Shop.

Lana said, "Here, Rick. These are yours and Jerry's new Glocks. I'm not supposed to give them to you until they are registered. Your old ones are registered, so I won't get in trouble if you don't tell anyone I gave them to you early. I thought you might need them."

"Thanks, Lana. That's nice of you."

She said, "Pammie asked me if you knew anything about doves, and I said I would ask you for her. She said if you did, would you go over to her house to check this one out that she hit with her car on the way home from work?"

I asked Lana for her address and phone number; she gave them to me. I told her I would call Pammie and go see what I could do after I finished with the case we are working on. We just have to get back to it because I have a feeling things are coming to a conclusion very soon.

Chapter

23

THINGS BEGIN TO POP

The next morning when I got up, I had this strange feeling that something was going to happen today I wouldn't like. I moped around, making me some SOS. I call it creamed chipped beef on toast. I got to liking it in the service. We had it about once a week.

I made me some coffee and sat at my dinette, looking out at the lake, eating my breakfast, and wishing I could go fishing. The lake looked as still as it can get, and that is when I love to fly-fish. The pop of the poppers attracts fish from a greater distance when the lake is calm like this.

I was sitting there, daydreaming, when a sheriff's car pulled up outside, and Bill Dade got out and knocked on the door. I hollered, "Come in."

He did and said, "Hello, Rick, I have some bad news for you. They called me last night to come out to investigate what looks like another murder up at the Blind Camp."

"Oh, no, who is it this time, Bill?"

"They think its Mary Contraire. Let's go up there and check it out. Do you and Jerry want to ride up there with me?"

"I'll call Jerry and ask him if he wants to go." I picked up my walkie-talkie and called Jerry; he answered right away.

I said, "Bill Dade and I are going up to the Blind Camp. Do you want to ride with him? I am. I'll explain everything to you on the way up there, okay?"

"Give me a minute," Jerry said, "and I'll be right over."

I asked Bill to give me a minute to change clothes. He said he would wait in the car. I took off what I had on, put on my leg holster, and tried my new Glock in it. It felt good I had purchased a new holster for the Glock, so I slid it into the holster to see if it was a good fit on my leg, and when I put on some slacks, you couldn't tell I had it on. The Glock was on the inside of my left leg, and the hold-out gun was on the right leg. I couldn't wear a shoulder holster because in Florida you hardly ever wear a coat or jacket. I put on a camp shirt to match the slacks, went outside to get into Bill's car, and waited until Jerry came around the corner of my motor home in a hurry. He knew something terrible had happened by the looks on our faces and us riding with Bill up there. He got in the back seat after speaking to Bill and me.

I turned around to tell Jerry what Bill had told me, and Bill said, "Let me start at the beginning and tell you and Jerry at the same time all I know about what happened."

"It seems that Archie got home late last night from Brandon, walked into his motor home, and found blood in the kitchen on the cabinet and floor. He called for Mary several times with no answer. He then went outside to check her car, and she wasn't in it. He went over to the office to see if anyone knew where she was. Long John was there, filling in for Peter while he was taking a few days off. Long John said he hadn't seen her yesterday. Archie called me and told me all I've told you. So here we are, going to check it out. Please let me do most of the talking while we are together at the camp."

"That's fine with me—and you too, Jerry?"

"Yeah, sure it is."

"I want us to give the motor home a good going over, and then I want you, Rick and Jerry, to do his car, boat, and her car. Also check around outside the motor home real good. Use gloves at all times. I want everything you find bagged, tagged; and a voucher form filled out, dated, and signed for."

We arrived, went around to Archie's motor home, and parked. Knocked on the door and soon heard footsteps. Archie was standing there in his undershorts. "Come on in while I go put some other shorts on," he said.

We went in and looked at the kitchen floor and all the blood. I got out a Ziploc bag, put in a sample of the blood, and marked it from the kitchen floor. I got out another bag, put in a sample of the blood off the cabinets, and marked it. I turned around and went into the front area to look around. I looked under the seats and furniture for anything interesting, but I saw nothing.

Archie came back out into the living area, and I went into the bathroom. I saw a hairbrush with some long hair, so I took some for another bag and marked it. I saw no blood in the bathroom, so I went into the bedroom. The bed was unmade; clothes were scattered around, but the room looked pretty clean. I started to leave the bedroom but stopped, and turned to look at a medium-size jewelry box. I opened it and rummaged through it until I found a large college ring like the one the mortician had described to me. I put it in a Ziploc bag, marked where it was found, then walked on out to the living room, where Bill and Jerry were taking finger-prints from all over the place.

I turned and walked outside to check Archie and Mary's cars. I looked under Archie's driver's seat and found a pair of pink panties and a used condom. No blood or anything else of importance. I reached for two more bags and found I was out. I went back in and asked Bill if he had anymore bags. He said no, but Archie said he had some and went and got them for me.

I went back out, put the condom in one bag, put the panties in another, and marked them. I popped the trunk and looked in it. Everything looked normal, with the exception of a bucket that had a little bit of reddish liquid in the bottom. I took out another Ziploc bag and put a little of the liquid in it. I flagged the bag, tagged it, vouched for it, and put it with the rest of the bags. I looked in her car and up under the sun visor found a picture of her and Archie kissing. I put that in another bag and did the same procedure. I found nothing else of value.

I turned to go over Archie's boat, and it wasn't there where it normally was. I went back in and asked him where it was.

He said, "I left it down at Camp Fins, because I was planning on going fishing in the morning."

"Why would you leave your boat down there when you could leave it tied up behind your motor home here? Doesn't Clyde charge you for putting in down there, and isn't it free to launch your boat here at this ramp?" Bill asked.

"Yes, but I was planning on fishing all along the south end of the lake in the morning. I like to fish down there better than anywhere else on the lake."

"Archie, with the bass boat and 100 Mercury you have on it, it would only take you five to ten minutes to run down there from here." Jerry said.

He just shrugged.

Jerry and I went back out and walked slowly around the motor home to the back and down to the bank of the pond. Right before I reached the bank, I saw a dark-red spot on the very edge of a stepping stone. I marked the spot with a little red flag I carry to murder scenes. I scraped some of the dark-red stuff off with my knife into one of my bags and marked it.

"Rick," Jerry said, "Again I don't think Archie did this. Why would a smart guy like him murder a lady who is babysitting his son for him in his own motor home and then call the cops? Why leave all the blood on his kitchen floor and on his cabinets? It just doesn't make sense to me."

We went back in the motor home; Bill said he was done questioning Archie. I told Bill and Jerry what I had accomplished and all I had found. I told Bill to take us back to the camp quickly. I wanted to get my boat so we could go down to Camp Fins and check out Archie's boat. Then we could come back up to the entrance to the pond at the Blind Camp and have a look see around there from the water.

Bill said, "Okay, sounds good to me."

Chapter

24

I DO BELIEVE WE ARE GETTING SOMEWHERE

When we got to my motor home, I went in and got a few things I thought I might need, like a big spotlight, et cetera, plus a cold six pack of Miller. Then we went on down to my boat. I handed each of them a cold beer. We all three got in, and I lowered us down in the water, cranked up, and backed out of my slip. I went at a slow speed until I was out in the lake, then I showered down on the motor and we went flying across the lake towards Camp Fins. The lake had just a slight ripple on it, so we skimmed across the water at a fast clip, and soon we were at the ramp at Camp Fins.

I asked Clyde the owner, if Archie's boat was here with him, and he said, "Yes it is."

"Clyde, will you show us where Archie's boat is?" I told him we wanted to check it out after telling him about the latest murder. He couldn't believe it.

He said, "Go ahead and have a look at it. If you need anything, please let me know."

We went over to Archie's boat and looked all around it first, and then I waded out along beside it a little ways. The water was shallow on each side of the canal so I could do so. I was looking around inside the boat some before getting into it to see what, if anything, I could see that might help us.

Most everything was in its place like the time I saw it sitting up in his yard there at the Blind Camp, with the exception of a boat cushion that had fallen out of the fishing chair up front and was lying on the deck. Other than that, the boat looked okay.

Bill said, "What are you thinking, Rick?"

"I'm comparing how it looked that day I saw the boat up at his place to how it looks now. That cushion lying on the deck is the only thing out of place."

I reached over and tilted it up. Under it was what looked like blood stains. I said, "Oh boy, look at this, Bill and Jerry. Look at these bloodstains."

They both looked and grinned real big. I then took out my knife to scrape up some of the blood to put some into one of my Ziploc bags. I bagged it, tagged it, and vouched for it.

"It looks like he cleaned the boat up but didn't pick up the cushion and didn't see the stains underneath," I said.

Bill said, "Let's take the boat back to Al's Ramp and Camp so Archie can't get to it to clean this off until we have it checked."

I checked the switch to see if the key was in it. It wasn't, so I turned to look for Clyde and saw him standing away off from us.

I hollered, "Clyde, did he leave a key with you?"

Clyde said, "No, he didn't, but I can hot-wire it for you if you want me too."

"That's great. Will you do it now?" Rick said.

He said, "Sure will," and took off for the office to get what he needed to do it.

Bill said, "I'll run Archie's boat back over to Al's camp, and you can tell Clyde what we are doing. Then I'll see you over there. Then we can run up to the Blind Camp by water, like you said, to look around."

While Jerry drove my bass boat back over to the camp, I said, "I think I will call

Barry and ask him if he will go back over to McGee's Funeral Home to question some of the employees about the case, Jerry."

"That's a terrific idea. Ask him to question any other family members other than Digger that work there also."

I called Barry at home, and he picked up on the first ring, which surprised me. I guess he was working at his desk, writing or something, and this is what I found out.

I said, "Barry, how are you feeling?"

"I'm doing a little better, Rick. I've had that flu that's going around, but I'm feeling much better today."

"Good, I'm glad to hear it. Listen, I wonder if you have time to do some more sleuthing for me. I need you to go over to McGee's Funeral Home and talk to some of the other family members if there is any who work there. Talk to some of the employees too. We need to find out if Archie's first wife was okay and not stepping out on him. We need to find something more on Mr. Archie.

I'll pay you something and pay your expenses if you'll let me."

"No, forget about it, Rick. I don't need the money. Besides, I'm glad to be able to help out a buddy. I need something to do anyway."

"Let me know when you have something I can use, okay?"

"I will. Don't worry, Okay."

Barry thought, Boy, am I glad to have something to keep me busy for a while. I think I'll go over and talk to the office manager about who all works or worked at McGee's during the time Archie's first wife went missing.

When I got to McGee's, I went in and told the lady at the front desk who I was and told her what I was working on.

She said, "My name is Fillie McGee. I'm the office manager and Digger's sister, and I would be glad to help you anyway I can."

I told her about finding the ring with Digger's help and about what we found out about it.

"I think you need to talk to Lily, who has worked for me for years," she said. "She hasn't been the same since you and Digger found that ring the other day. She must have overheard you two talking about it. She's been moping around here, acting like she is guilty of something herself."

"Do you think she would like to have lunch with me?"

"She has a steady boyfriend and might turn you down. She brings her lunch anyway. I'll introduce you to her, and you can talk to her in her office. Is that okay with you?"

"That's fine with me."

Fillie took me to Lily's office, and I handed her my card, shook her hand, and told her I was Barry Greer.

She said, "It's nice to meet you. What can I do for you?"

"I want to talk to you about Archie Crabtree and the day his wife went missing a few years back. If it's all right I would like to record our conversation."

"Yes, that will be fine with me."

"I'm Barry Greer, and I'm talking to Lily White." I said that for the benefit of the recorder.

"Oh, I'm so glad someone finally has come to investigate Mrs. Crabtree's disappearance.

"What do you know that might help us out with this case, Lily?"

"Not much, but I do know one thing that might help. My boyfriend came by for me after work and took me out to dinner. When we returned, I noticed the crematory was smoking, but didn't pay that much attention, figuring it had been used by Mr. McGee or one of the other employees. The next day is when they found that it had been used the day before by persons unknown. They cleaned it out and found the ring."

"Thanks, Lily that might help some."

Chapter

25

I SMELL A PAYCHECK

*B*y this time Jerry had just pulled us into the slip at Al's, and Bill was waiting on us. I raised us up to dock level, and Bill got in, and I got each of us the last of the Miller High Life. Then I let us down again, and away we went up toward the Blind Camp. It was dark, but not as dark as it could have been, because as

I looked over my left shoulder toward the western sky, I saw a crescent moon that gave off a little light, so it wasn't total dark.

I cut off the outboard, tilted it up, and went up front. I sat in the front fishing chair, put the trolling motor over, stepped on the foot pedal, and quietly trolled into the pond right up behind Archie's backdoor.

I pointed out to Bill and Jerry the drop of dark red on the stepping stone beside the little red flag I had stuck there earlier. We looked all around but saw nothing else. I turned, went back out into the lake, and trolled toward Rosa Lee Creek on the north end.

By now we were quite a ways from the Blind Camp, so I pulled up the trolling motor, went back to the driver's seat, turned the switch key to start the outboard, and ran us about five hundred yards farther east to the same area where I had been surrounded by gators. There is a little inlet there in the reed line, so I cut off the outboard again and put back over the trolling motor.

I got out my spotlight and plugged it into the place where the cigarette lighter goes. I shined all around the opening of that little inlet in the reeds, but I didn't see anything at first until we got a little farther inside the small cove.

Then I began to see pairs of red eyes looking at us from all around that area. That bright spotlight really made those red gator eyes stand out.

This cove is alive with alligators. I eased in a little more, shined my spotlight around, and saw something hanging on some reeds on the left. I had no idea what it could be, but I carefully eased over to it anyway and reached over the side very carefully to retrieve it. I held it up to the light and spread it out so I could see what it was. Then I realized I was holding the torn and dirty negligee Mary had been wearing when Jerry and I went to see Archie what seemed like a week ago.

I handed the negligee to Jerry, and he grimaced, remembering how good she looked to us at the door that day. I shined my spotlight around some more and saw red eyes shining at us from all directions. Frogs were croaking so loud, I could hardly hear, and the smells were horrific. Some gators were croaking too, and mosquitoes by the millions buzzed around our heads and sucked our blood. I was itching and scratching all over.

I thought I saw something else a bit farther on into the darkness ahead. Man, this place was alive with gators and stinks is not the word for it. I thought it must be a hatchery, with beds everywhere. Lying up on a thick patch of weeds and water hyacinths was what looked like some blonde hair, all bloody. And something else... that was bloody... was attached to the hair.

I put on a pair of rubber gloves and trolled in a little more until we were right up against the weed patch. I shined my spotlight all over that bunch of weeds to see if it would be safe to stick my hand over to retrieve what we had seen. I didn't see any eyes looking back at me right there, so I very carefully reached over and grabbed the hair, as I was pulling it up the water exploded, I saw the snout and then the head of him coming up after the prize I had. A huge gator with his mouth wide open was going to stop his treasure from being stolen. He snapped his jaws shut just under my hand and sank back in the water. He splashed his tail down so hard, it sounded like lightning during a storm. He had just missed the hair and my hand by a hair. Then I saw that something came up with the hair; it..... Was what was left of Mary's head?

I put the head in the bottom of the boat real quick, turned us around, yanked up that trolling motor, and started the outboard. I revved it up and tore out of there as fast as the boat would take us.

I went back down to our camp and went into my slip faster than I ever had before. I raised the boat up to dock level, reached over, and got this five-gallon bucket I use to take fish out of my boat to clean them at the sinks provided for that purpose. I put Mary's head in it and covered it with a rag; covered it so no one could see.

I turned to look at the guys. All three of us were scratching like crazy. We all had red, itchy bumps all over our faces, necks, and arms. All I could say was, "Wheeeew!"

Bill said, "Quickly, let's go back up to the Sun n' Fun Blind Camp to arrest Archie before he kills somebody else."

I wanted to laugh but knew better. I just said, "Yeah, let's hurry."

We went up to the Blind Camp, pulled into the area near Archie's motor home, knocked on the door, and waited. I knocked again and waited. No answer.

Bill said, "Quick, Rick, run around to the other side to see if he is going out a window or something."

I reached down, pulled up my pants leg to get my Glock, cocked it, ran around the front of the motor home, and saw Archie trying to go out the driver's side door.

I pointed my Glock at Archie and said, "Freeze Archie, you are under arrest!"

He froze, and I told him to lean and spread against the side of the motor home. As he was making the move to lean on the side of the motorhome, his hand came out from under his shirt with a pistol, and he fired at me.

I heard one bullet whistle by my left ear, felt another sting my left ear, and took one in the left side. He pulled the trigger before I could fire my first shot, which hit him in the chest.

I fired one more, and then he fell and started rolling around, while I was falling over a short hedge. I was rolling around, trying to get another shot, when I heard two more shots.

I looked up and over at the back corner of the motor home, and there was Jerry with his new Glock, pointed and ready to fire again if necessary. By this time Bill came around back to see what all the shooting was about.

Bill said, "Boy, it sounded like you guys had started a war back here for a while there."

"The sucker shot at me three times before I could get off my first round," I said. I hit him in the chest twice, and he still had fight in him. He missed with his first try and then hit my left ear and left side. It looks like Jerry saved my life with his two shots. We both hit him two times each.

He will never rape and kill another blonde woman again. We have the goods on this S-O-B now. We punched his ticket for him almost for good, didn't we, Jerry?"

Bill called an ambulance for me. I told him to have them come for me at Al's Ramp and Camp.

Jerry and Bill stuffed Archie Crabtree into the backseat of Bill's police car. It has a cage separating the back from the front. When we finally got back down to my motor home, I asked Bill to get all the Ziploc bags and stuff I had gathered, plus the five-gallon bucket, and he put it all in his trunk.

I said to Bill, "Don't forget to have DNA tests done on the panties, condom, negligee, and blood at all the places where we found it. And check up on the ring I found. I think you'll find Archie was wearing it when he hit his wife, Linda, in the left temple with it."

"Don't worry. I won't forget," he said. "I'll have Sarah mail you your money; mail me all your expense receipts, and she will mail you a check for that too. Thanks a whole heap for your help, boys. I couldn't have done it without you. I think they will take you to Lake Wales Hospital to patch you up, Rick. Have them send me the bill for that too."

I said, "Thanks, and I'll mail you that tape Barry made of Lily White's statement when it comes. Do you want a cold Miller High Life for the road, Bill?"

He said, "Thanks, but I better not. I've still got to get this turkey locked up and maybe get some medical attention for him. Then I have all the paperwork to do. See you soon."

"We enjoyed working for you, Sheriff Dade. I'm looking forward to seeing you soon too."